Reasonable Doubt

Reasonable Doubt

by Joel Bernbaum,
Lancelot Knight,
and Yvette Nolan

Playwrights Canada Press
Toronto

Jacket art and design by Chief Lady Bird
Author photo of Joel Bernbaum © Matt Ramage
Author photo of Lancelot Knight © Matt Ramage
Author photo of Yvette Nolan © Keesic Douglas

Playwrights Canada Press
202-269 Richmond St. W., Toronto, ON M5V 1X1
416.703.0013 | info@playwrightscanada.com | www.playwrightscanada.com

For professional or amateur production rights, please contact Playwrights Canada Press.

LIBRARY AND ARCHIVES CANADA CATALOGUING IN PUBLICATION
Title: Reasonable doubt / Joel Bernbaum, Lancelot Knight, and Yvette Nolan.
Names: Bernbaum, Joel, author. | Knight, Lancelot, author. | Nolan, Yvette, author.
Description: A play.
Identifiers: Canadiana (print) 2022020912X | Canadiana (ebook) 20220209197
  | ISBN 9780369103604 (softcover) | ISBN 9780369103628 (PDF)
  | ISBN 9780369103611 (HTML)
Classification: LCC PS8603.E73525 R43 2022 | DDC c812/.6—dc23

Playwrights Canada Press operates on land which is the ancestral home of the Anishinaabe Nations (Ojibwe / Chippewa, Odawa, Potawatomi, Algonquin, Saulteaux, Nipissing, and Mississauga), the Wendat, and the members of the Haudenosaunee Confederacy (Mohawk, Oneida, Onondaga, Cayuga, Seneca, and Tuscarora), as well as Métis and Inuit peoples. It always was and always will be Indigenous land.

We acknowledge the support of the Canada Council for the Arts, the Ontario Arts Council (OAC), Ontario Creates, and the Government of Canada for our publishing activities.

For seven generations and forward.

Introduction
by Maria Campbell

It was a beautiful sunny afternoon when I pulled up to the little house and shut the motor off. "Do you think she's home?" I asked my aunt.

"Well let's go in and see," Aunty said, getting out of the car and stretching after the long drive. "Somebody could have picked her up. She loves going for drives."

"I think she's home." I pointed to the smoke coming from the chimney.

"You're right," Aunty laughed, "and she's probably got a pot of tea on and knows we're here. That's the kind of old lady she is."

"She" was Mary Pimee, the widowed wife of Horse Child, son of Mistahi Maskwa, Big Bear, chief of what the old people have always called Big Bear's band. Big Bear was a beloved and respected leader who was charged and imprisoned for his alleged involvement in the 1885 Resistance in the Battlefords. Little did I know how much "She" was going to change my life.

I followed Aunty to the house, stopping to pat a lazy old dog who slowly got up to check us out, sniffing and licking our hands, then plopping herself back down in the sun. I chuckled as Aunty knocked on the door. That was just the kind of dog I knew Mary would have.

"Come in," a voice called. Aunty pushed the door open and we walked in.

"ay hay, tânisi nôsimak, hello granddaughters."

Mary was sitting across the room on a metal cot, looking not at all like I had imagined. She was very "old time," with skinny little braids hanging to her shoulders under the floral blue scarf wrapped, old style, around her head. She had on a faded green dress, a much-patched blue sweater, wraparound moccasins, and rubbers on her little feet. And on her lap, a beautiful and bright crazy quilt.

Her face lit up when she recognized my aunty, who took her hand and shook it, bending down to kiss her. They visited for a time, talking about the weather, relatives, and then my aunty introduced me. She told Mary I was there to ask her for âcimowina, stories about the old days, and what it was like when she was young.

"nêhiyawêw ana," my aunty said. "She speaks Cree." The old lady smiled at me.

Mary had piercing black eyes and I felt like she saw into every part of me as she took my hand and stroked it. "nôsim," she murmured, "granddaughter." She patted a place beside her on the bed. "I have been waiting for you."

I sat down on the bed and I was instantly comfortable with her. She had been waiting for me; that's what old people say when they connect with you. That's what my nohkoms always said, and that's how it was with the old ladies I worked with. "I have been waiting for you."

"Now tell me," she said, "why do you want to know what it was like when I was young?" Her eyes twinkled, and that was the beginning of our relationship.

I spent many days visiting with her over that summer and I was able to write an article for *Maclean's* magazine that was published in 1975. It was just a very tiny story from the larger one she told me, but she didn't want me to publish the whole story because she was afraid. Afraid she would expose her family and people to danger and violence.

"Who would believe me?" she asked. "An old Indian woman, who was supposed to die a long time ago. Those White people would be so angry and I would just stir up trouble for everybody."

I understood her fear. I'd grown up with old people who whispered when they talked about the old days. Always sure that the police or the soldiers would come and take them away. Put them in jail or maybe even hang them or the people they loved. And I also knew from personal experience that no matter what White people said, they didn't really want to hear those stories. I had just had two pages pulled from my first book, my publisher fearing he would get sued if he published what I had written, and that I, too, might be sued or even go to prison.

And so, I promised Mary I would put her story away, along with the photographs she had allowed me to take. I put everything into a box and into storage. Eventually, I forgot which box I had stored it in. That was forty-two years ago.

As I write this, we are nearing the two-year mark of isolation and restrictions due to the global pandemic, COVID-19. Everyone has their story about the way they have passed through this period, and mine involves time spent pulling material out of storage: old boxes full of writing and interview transcripts of the many old people I have worked with and have been mentored by for over sixty years. Some of those old people were in their nineties and older at the time I visited with them. Mary Pimee was not sure of her age when I met her. Her people say she was over a hundred years old ikospê kâ kîwêt when she went home.

It is important here to understand about reciprocity and its role in the transmission of Indigenous knowledge, be it stories, songs, ceremonies, or sacred objects. On that first visit, I gave Mary a pouch of tobacco, four metres of cloth, a purple silk scarf, and a box of groceries. Then I became her helper/student.

This essay is the first of many âcimowina, small stories that she shared with me. Those stories gave me a context and shaped the work I would be doing and how I would do it, and that work continues to this day. This sounds simple enough, but isn't. It is only now that I can see it. âcimowina have work to do, and we as students of âcimowina do not always have a choice. The story comes when it is time to do its work.

When Joel asked me to write an essay to accompany *Reasonable Doubt*, I didn't know for sure what I was going to do. I only knew that to even begin to understand where the horrific racism and hate came from in this province—which spilled out during the Stanley trial—we have to understand the foundations that Saskatchewan and Canada were built on. The treaties, for example, were accepted by Indigenous peoples because they had to survive. They had no other options and they saw treaties as a way to secure a future for their peoples, who were dying from epidemics and starvation. It is well known and documented, however, that the dominion used this crisis to "control, isolate and eliminate" Indigenous peoples to make way for colonial settlement.* As James Daschuk has written, the state used starvation and disease to "clear the plains" of Indigenous peoples** and the treaties were their way to deal with Indigenous peoples "who were perceived as an obstacle to settlement."***

I started to write about that period for this introduction, and of course it didn't work. Then one day I opened a box and inside was Mary's photograph and all my notes and some transcripts. It worked. So here she is: "ê-kî nipayi-ayimahk," she began. "It was very hard."

"When I think about it there is only death and pain. My childhood was one of hunger. I was—we were—always hungry, us children. So hungry our bellies hurt and swelled up, just like the ones you see on TV in those Black countries. We ate whatever we found, whatever was given to us. Mostly it was rotten meat . . . dead rotting horses and dogs, rancid rotting salt pork and flour, so full of bugs and worms that the flour moved. We ate grass and roots. That was probably the healthiest food we had. People were dead and dying all around us. We were so hungry, us children, we would search the bodies for food.

"We were always moving, piyisk ê-kî-papâmipiciyahk. At first it was with our horses and dogs, but as the hunger became worse, we killed them, ate them, and walked, carrying what little we owned on our backs.

"Once we children saw an old buffalo cow in a coulee not far from the river and we ran back to the camp screaming, 'paskwâwi mostosak takohtêwak,' the buffalo are back! No one believed us, saying they were all gone. Finally, Big Bear himself and one of his young men followed us. The cow was laying under some willows. The young man had a gun and was going to shoot her, but Big Bear said, 'kiya, pakitin

---

* Andrew Woolford, "Ethnic Cleansing, Canadian Style," in *Clearing the Plains: Disease, Politics of Starvation and the Loss of Indigenous Life* by James E. Daschuk (Regina: University of Regina Press, 2019), 232.

** James E. Daschuk, *Clearing the Plains: Disease, Politics of Starvation and the Loss of Indigenous Life* Regina: University of Regina Press, 2019).

*** Woolford, 232.

ka-pimātisitpimâtisit. No, let her live. She is more pitiful than we are. She has no family to mourn her.'"

Mary was quiet for a long time and I reached for her quilt to cover her. I thought she had fallen asleep, but she waved it away.

"Mistahi Maskwa, Big Bear, was a good man. He had strong pawâkanak, and he knew medicine. We children all loved him very much and respected him. He was kind and generous with us, as he was with all people.

"Once, we were running from the soldiers and we came to a river. The soldiers were very close and Mistahi Maskwa stopped and raised his hand. We stopped too, thinking he saw something we didn't. He sang a song, and as he sang a thick mist rolled behind us and formed a wall between us and the soldiers. We were able to cross the river and walk for several hours until he was sure we had lost them and the men had found a safe place for us to camp.

"But in the end even his pawâkanak and power were not enough to help us. So, one morning the people had a meeting and his daughter told him they had to go back. Turn themselves in to the soldiers because if they didn't there would be no more children. Several had died during the night."

Mary told me that she believed she was about eight years old when Wandering Spirit and the warriors were hanged in Battleford. She was there, along with other children and adults from the reserves and the residential school. They were forced to watch the hanging so they would learn to be good Indians.

"How could we forget?" she said. "It was so quiet. Even yôtin, the wind was still. We heard their necks snap."

After Mary said this, she was still again for a long time. I remember getting up to make her a cup of tea, trying to be strong. But even now as I write this, I feel her pain.

Later, as we prepared our supper, she told me that Wandering Spirit and the men who died with him had killed the priest and those men because they had raped and abused the women and young girls for many years. Those men wouldn't give rations to the starving people unless they serviced them first and they had a place in the storeroom for that. Often they even demanded that the little girls be given to them and they would play with them sexually in exchange for food.

"namôya wihkâc niya. It never happened to me because I was not pretty. Many little girls were taught how to make themselves ugly."

Mary then told me that Wandering Spirit and some of the men had gone to the police, but nothing was ever done. They had finally gone to that priest, Fafard, and begged him to help. But he did nothing either, saying that the women teased and tempted the men.

"This was not true. It was never true," she said.

"We were good people, but it didn't matter. They hated us and nobody could do anything."

What Mary said that day was so painful, but can perhaps bring some hope as we struggle through the ongoing injustice represented in the Stanley trial. And so, I will end with the words she shared in her âcimowina.

"It will be a long time yet before anybody can do anything. The White man is very powerful, but one day he will have no power. ekwanma manitow wiyinikwin, that is Creator's law."

Maria Campbell is a Métis writer, playwright, filmmaker, scholar, teacher, community organizer, activist, and elder. Halfbreed is regarded as a foundational work of Indigenous literature in Canada. She has authored several other books and plays, and has directed and written scripts for a number of films. She has also worked with Indigenous youth in community theatre and advocated for the hiring and recognition of Indigenous people in the arts. She has mentored many Indigenous artists during her career, established shelters for Indigenous women and children, and run a writers' camp at the national historical site at Batoche, where every summer she produces commemorative events on the anniversary of the battle of the 1885 North-West Resistance. Maria Campbell is an officer of the Order of Canada and holds five honorary doctorates.

The Process
by Joel Bernbaum and Yvette Nolan

Genesis

In February 2020, Saskatoon's Persephone Theatre produced the premiere production of *Reasonable Doubt*, a documentary play with music created by Joel Bernbaum, Lancelot Knight, and Yvette Nolan. The events upon which *Reasonable Doubt* was based—the shooting death of Colten Boushie, a young Cree man, and the acquittal of White farmer Gerald Stanley—had already divided the province, and the creative team wanted to engender understanding and empathy, not further drive a wedge between communities.

This project began in 2015. Joel had had a great experience making *Home Is a Beautiful Word*—a documentary play about homelessness—which premiered at the Belfry Theatre in Victoria, BC, in 2014. That play showed him the true power of community engagement; Joel wanted to return home and make a documentary play about Indigenous and non-Indigenous relations in Saskatchewan. The Saskatchewan Arts Board funded the first fifty interviews. The conversations were interesting, but very polite. It was important to keep talking to people about this topic, and Joel was thankful that Persephone Theatre saw the value of continuing the conversations and decided to commission a full play. Joel kept doing interviews.

Then, on August 9, 2016, Colten Boushie was shot and killed on the Stanley farm in west-central Saskatchewan. This tragic event rocked our whole province. Joel kept doing interviews, but they were different now. People were speaking with a new kind of raw honesty. People wanted to talk. People needed to talk. Interviews were transcribed and Yvette began pouring over thousands of pages of transcripts. Joel and Lancelot would sift through transcripts and see how they became songs. We worked together with the hopes of capturing a kaleidoscope of views about this incident, this province, and our people.

It was our hope that this play created a bigger conversation: an opportunity for us to talk to each other, and with each other, and to talk about what has happened on this land and how we can live together in a good way. It would be uncomfortable at times, but we felt it was worth it.

The Engagement

From the beginning of this project we knew audience engagement would be crucial. To us, audience engagement offers the general public "ways in" to the play. Ways that make them participants and not just consumers. This participation is made possible through relationship-building. The verbatim theatre form lends itself to engagement with the public because the interviewer already has relationships with the interview subjects. Joel reached out to the Boushie family and the Stanley family to ask them to participate in the interview process. The Boushie family agreed to participate and the Stanley family declined. Joel continued to communicate with the Boushie family and as many interviewees as possible to get their artistic and ethical approval. In order to engage the general public we decided to invite people into the process of making the play. Yvette opened up the rehearsal hall and on several occasions we arranged for visitors to come and watch the actors work. The visitors ranged from local media personalities to the mayor to a class of grade eight students.

We also wanted to ensure that a wide range of community leaders attended an open rehearsal, so we used relationships in the community to invite people who were already doing work on Indigenous/non-Indigenous relations to attend. We had hoped fifteen to twenty people would attend. We were excited to run out of chairs when over sixty people packed the rehearsal room that day. After watching forty-five minutes of work, Joel hosted a question-and-answer period in the lobby. Those people became informal ambassadors for the production, armed with an emotional attachment to the play and connected to information about the audience engagement during the run.

During the run we worked with Lisa Bayliss, Persephone Theatre's marketing director, to coordinate facilitated audience discussions after every performance. Over a hundred people stayed each night to share their reactions and experience to the play. Lisa also worked with the Saskatchewan Human Rights Commission to coordinate two different "Courageous Conversation" panels before two different performances. These events were both standing-room only. The run of the show completely sold out. We believe the audience engagement work fuelled both the box-office success and the community impact of the play.

The Weave

We knew that Lancelot's music was going to be a critical part of *Reasonable Doubt*. The material was so hard—hard truths spoken by real people about living together on this land—that audiences needed the music to create space to breathe and reflect. When words spoken by characters hurt too much, the company would sing, or listen to Lancelot sing. The words that were like weapons coming out of a character's mouth somehow were more palatable, comprehensible, even comforting, when set to music.

We did not know, when we began the project, that we would eventually be weaving together not only the interviews of Saskatchewanians and Lancelot's music, but also the trial transcripts from the murder trial of a White man who shot a Cree youth on his property.

Once we had the three strands of the braid, the dramaturgy of the piece became the crux around which to achieve some kind of balance. How do we tell this story on behalf of a community? How do we honour all those people who trusted us with their words?

Not everyone was satisfied, not everyone was happy with the result, but those who came stayed through to the end, and those who spoke often spoke about how fair they felt the play was in its portrayal of a community.

Postscript

When we closed this show we did not know it would be the last play we did in a long time. We did not yet know the severity of COVID-19. We did not yet know the name George Floyd. Now we are uncertain of when we will be able to do this play again. We are certain that this play is even more relevant than ever. In a time where we re-evaluate what it means to be together/apart there is no more important task than building relationships with each other.

Reasonable Doubt was commissioned by Persephone Theatre, with initial interviews funded by the Saskatchewan Arts Board, with assistance from the National Arts Centre Collaborations and the Saskatchewan Playwrights Centre. The play was first produced by Persephone Theatre at the Rawlco Radio Hall Main Stage, Saskatoon, on January 29, 2020, with the following cast and creative team:

Kris Alvarez: Ensemble
Nathan Howe: Ensemble
Lancelot Knight: Ensemble
Krystle Pederson: Ensemble
Tara Sky: Ensemble
Colin Wolf: Ensemble

Joel Bernbaum: Co-Creator/Interviewer/Editor
Lancelot Knight: Co-Creator/Composer/Sound Designer
Yvette Nolan: Co-Creator/Director/Dramaturg

Katey Wattam: Assistant Director
Carla Orosz: Set Designer
Jensine Emeline: Assistant Set Designer
Byron Hnatuk: Lighting Designer
Taegan O'Bertos: Costume and Projection Designer
Laura Kennedy: Stage Manager
Ricardo Alvarado: Assistant Stage Manager

Mackenzie Dawson, Paige Goodman, Jonelle Gunderson, Lauren Holfeuer, Jenna-Lee Hyde, and Megan Zong: Transcribers

Notes

The play alternates between three worlds:
the courtroom,
the interviews,
and the songs.

Six actors shift between all roles.

They all play instruments and sing during the songs.

Song lyrics are in bold.

There is also underscored live music at times.

Identifying information about each speaker is projected onto
the set.

A Note on Transcription

Verbatim theatre is an art, not a science, so readers are encouraged to discover the voice and thoughts of the speakers through the punctuated transcription. There is no one way to transcribe for verbatim theatre, but it is important that transcribers and actors use the same transcription key. All interviews were transcribed by human transcribers using the transcription key below.

Transcription Key

Coughs/sighs = indicated with brackets: "really think than (*coughs twice*) *cuh cuh*"

Emphasis volume increase = in SMALL CAPS: "LOVE YOU"

Interruption = —

Stutter = -

Short pause (three seconds or less) = . . .

Long pause (more than three seconds) = ...

Laughter or singing = indicated with italics: "*uh huh huh*"

Act One

Scene 1—Court

DAN, sixties, White.

DAN: I'm from North Battleford, Saskatchewan, and uh . . . Uhh I attended them all. Every day. I was, you know, a seeker in the truth in this whole thing, right? An' so I decided to go to all the preliminary hearings and caught myself with a spot in there. I wanted to know—I wanted to know what it really was that went on out there that day . . . y'know?

JUDGE, sixties, White.
DENNY, fifties, Indigenous.

DENNY holds an eagle feather.

The eagle feather appears several times throughout the play.

JUDGE: Sir, I notice you have an eagle feather there.

DENNY: Yes.

JUDGE: Would you be kind enough to explain to me the-the purpose and what that would be?

DENNY: This eagle feather here represents the truth and justice.

JUDGE: Okay.

DAN: They brought a piece of the Native culture into the courtroom. He brought in eagle feathers, okay? We're on day three and uh the judge brings up the thing about the eagle feathers. And asks him some questions about it. And this is in the absence of the jury.

DENNY: When you walked in here, I honoured you by lifting this eagle feather. And as they walk in, I honour the jury also—

JUDGE: Okay. Do you—

DENNY: —for justice and truth.

JUDGE: Do you mind if I tell them that?

DENNY: Sure, you can.

JUDGE: Okay. That way, everyone knows what it is. I-I presumed it was something along those lines, and I think it would be appropriate to tell them that so that they're aware of-of what it is that you're doing. Does that work for you, sir?

DENNY: Sure.

DAN: My thoughts were right away, ohh, don't go there, Judge, don't go there with that like, you're a smart enough man to recognize culture and-and maybe just like do you need to be asking this, y'know? Anyway, Denny was good enough to tell 'em, yes sir, it's to honour you and the jury in your search for truth and justice, in the courtroom, right?

JUDGE: I hope everyone is well. Typical Saskatchewan February 1st day. I'm glad to see that everyone has strong batteries in their car and is able to make it. I am just going to mention one thing.

There is a gentleman in the—if you'd just stand up, sir? When I walked in, he has an eagle feather, and he-he kind of nodded it at me. And then I noticed that he's done that with you. And I asked him what it was about, and what he told me is that he's honouring me and the jury by doing that. So I thought I would just find out what that was about, and he was kind enough to explain it to me.

DAN: And he left it at that . . . and I went . . . but you didn't tell him everything the man says?! The man said . . . in the search for truth and justice. You people . . . in your search for truth and justice.

JUDGE: So in case you were curious, you know what the answer is, too. Thank you very much, sir.

DAN: So we had a thing here with symbolism, right, and he was to explain what the symbolism of the eagle feathers was so I thought, well then . . . if this court is kinda like a show we have to explain how 'bout the judge explain why thee . . . himself and-and the defence, y'know, attorney, and the crown prosecutor puts on special garments when they're, y'know, they have a cloak they put, and they have a white tie that comes down and-and so I'm going, what's the explanation of that?! So I googled it an' I found out why they dress this way . . . it represented sobriety or straight-thinking . . . it also is to say that those-those men there will bring us together . . . in an honourable way, and the people they are and the learned men that they are . . . they are looking for truth and justice. And so I said, well ya know this morning . . . both of you were looking for the same thing. One was eagle feathers, the other was the way . . . these men of the court were dressed.

Scene 2—Saskatoon Is . . .

Song: "The Place Where We Grow Up."

ALL: Saskatoon is

BRYAN, forties, White.

BRYAN: Uh. I'd have to say Saskatoon is changing.

JULIA, thirties, White.

ALL: Saskatoon is

JULIA: a wonderful place, a warm city, a sprawling city, um a city of lots of rural folks coming together to try and figure out how to have a city.

ALL: Saskatoon is

ANNA, seventies, Indigenous.

ANNA: the sky and the light and the smell of the river to me, and uh . . . I have never been happier anyplace else. There's something about the land that's just so—it's so uh—it's-it's very gentle, but it's really strong.

**The smell of the river, and the stars on the beautiful night.
The grass in September and the ember skyline.**

**The place where we grew up
The place where we come from
The place we grow up
. . . Where we belong**

BERT, fifties, Indigenous.

BERT: Saskatoon is uh a-a vibrant, beautiful city. We're always in the news for the wrong reasons but-but uh and we're—and we're never in the news enough for the right reasons. People are ah almost like small-town but it-it uh . . . that-that farmer mentality. If somebody needs a hand you just walk over and give 'em a hand.

Treaty 6, Dene, Cree, and the homeland of the Métis
A place of new-found dreams where families run deep

The place where we come from
The place where you grew up
The place where we come from
Where we belong

> ANGEL, *thirties, Indigenous.*

ANGEL: Saskatoon is a place for me for growing and opportunity and also it's a place for . . . learning on both sides of injustice and justice relationship uhm . . . let's see how can I put this . . . of being violent and non-violent. Race-race-racism uhm poverty, gang violence, homelessness, uhm single parents, people dyin', people livin'.

People living, people dying, people moving to this place
Always trying, nodding at a familiar face

The place where we grew up
The place where we come from
The place we grow up
. . . Where we belong

> NOEL, *twenties, Indigenous.*

NOEL: Saskatoon is fractured. It's very uhm . . . beautiful as a whole, but there is this great line that goes down the centre of it an'-an' bisects uh the community. And I mean it's not only just the river it's the lines within our tribal understandings of who is in our-our-our village, who is in our community. Who are in the places that we care about and the places that we don't care about we find the others.

PHILLIP, *sixties, White.*

PHILLIP: Saskatoon is not going the direction which I think would be beneficial for people living in harmony, just an example Race Relations Committee used to be called Living in Harmony. And it's shifted towards anti-racism—which already implies that there is division, that there is uh . . . conflict.

**Every night you'll hear a different language if you listen along
Out in the cold so many people living a tragic song**

FELIX, *forties, White.*

FELIX: The colour of my skin is something I've never really thought of, but it's an important part of who I am and-and maybe impacts me more than I realize so yeah.

ANNA: The colour of my skin is brown, it's not real brown, it's kind of uh . . . middle brown, I guess. It's the colour of-of the-of the grass in uh early September, late August. And it's uh . . . I think it's a very gentle colour, and so I think about gentleness.

**The place where we grew up
The place where we come from
The place we grow up
. . . Where we belong**

Scene 3—Opening Statements

Music continues underneath.

DEFENCE, *fifties, White.*
CROWN, *fiftes, White.*

DEFENCE: Colten Boushie's death is a tragedy. There is no doubt about that. And we can never lose sight of that.

CROWN: We will be calling a variety of kinds of evidence.

DEFENCE: This is really not a murder case at all. This is a case about what can go terribly wrong when you create a situation which is really in the nature of a home invasion. For farm people, your yard is your castle.

CROWN: Colten Boushie was in a vehicle when he—when he was shot.

DEFENCE: What we have here is we have a family. And Gerry—Gerry didn't go looking for trouble on August 9th, 2016. He was doing what he does every day. He was working on his ranch.

CROWN: You will hear that he died of a gunshot wound.

DEFENCE: Ultimately, ultimately, this case comes down to a freak accident that occurred in the course of an unimaginably scary situation one afternoon.

The place where we grew up
The place where we come from
The place we grow up
. . . Where we belong

Scene 4—Race Narratives

A grade five classroom

CLOE, *eleven, White.*
TOM, *ten, White.*
RUBY, *eleven, White.*
JORDAN, *ten, White.*

CLOE: Race is your cultural heritage.

TOM: Race is your skin colour.

RUBY: Race is can also effect how people look at you and how they like trust you an'—just because that you look different. Like soo ...say...Donald Trump thinks all Mexicans are like terrorists ev-bu—just because they're from Mexico.

JORDAN: I think race is something that causes a lot a conflict between people and communities.

Rural Saskatchewan.

ROSE *and* RALPH, *seventies, White.*

ROSE: (*smacks lips*) Predominately a lot of German people here. Uhh...but in the last while we've had...peo—other nationalities moving in. We've got ahh...restaurant downtown that's operated by a Chinese lady, uh...the Red Bull is now operated by people from Korea, South Korea. And uh...yeah so, and we've-we've got some Native people living here, y'know. They're either adopted kids or—

RALPH: VERY few though!

(*overlapping*) Jus'-just the small small thing. And-and there's no reserves around here.

ROSE: (*overlapping*) Very few yeah! There is-is a few yeah. Yeah.

RALPH: We should make mention, ORIGINALLY this area was preDOMINANTly German with a-wid a nice mixture of Ukrainians. They called the offsprings Geranians. (*laughs*) *Heh heh heh heh heh heh.* But-but now as Rose had mentioned because the influx of new people and affordable housing. Uh . . . there's a lot of . . .

ROSE: Intermarriages! We have a little bit of everything here right now. Well intermarriages, you know. The women are Native and their children are Native . . . living with a White. There's about three-three Native families here in town. That I can think of—

RALPH: PARTIAL Natives! (*laughs*) *Heh heh.*

A grade five classroom

SAM, eleven, White.
RUBY, eleven, White.

SAM: The whole uhm whole Colten Boushie Gerald Stanley thing uhm . . . I don't really have a side exactly uhm yeah. Colten Boushie was-was an'-and some friends were really drunk and then they went—they were going around an making mischief and then Gerald Stanley I guess was trying to protect his family and-an' shot Colten Boushie.

RUBY: I think skin colour DID matter, but it SHOULDN'T have mattered. Because ehm like I dunno, if it was a White man, he might not have been shot because a lot o—that's another stereotype, a lot of Indig-Indigenous people like ON the streets are . . . assumed to be dangerous.

KAT, eleven, White.

KAT: I was . . . listening as my dad and his girlfriend fought about it. Uhm . . . 'cause they both disagreed about if he was guilty or not and uhm . . . my dad was saying that he wasn't and that he was just doing it to protect his home and family and because they WERE trying to steal something from him, well that's what he said, that they were trying to steal like his truck or his quad or something an' his girlfriend said well, if someone was coming for your quad would you have . . . the guts to shoot him? And he said yeah! I paid a lot of money for that!

Rural Saskatchewan.

RALPH: This will stand out as one of the four uh . . . significant trials ever held in this province. And of course, the first one was Louis R-Riel way back when and then it was Colin Thatcher uh . . . Robert Latimer, and then this one. And uh . . . y'know I-I didn't realize that I was f-front row seat to such a historic trial. You had to shake your head once in a while to realize this is the real thing. History was unfolding it-itself before your eyes. What we found interesting in fact I'm going to share this with you ahh . . . is that I had Gerald Stanley's father phoned me here a couple days ago. Friday evening.

ROSE: Well you're jumping ahead now.

RALPH: Yes! I'm jumping ahead! He phoned me to thank ahh me an'-an' Rose and our son that was attending our family for support-ing them. But here is something that he shared with me and that is that after the first couple days of trial.

ROSE: Is that to be shared, I wonder?

RALPH: I think so! Because I mean you will decide how to decipher it. Is that . . . the *StarPhoenix* wasn't doing justice to the coverage. He said—

Speaking at the same time:

ROSE: (*overlapping*) He felt it was one-sided.

RALPH: (*overlapping*) He said VERY one-sided!

INITIALLY came out that these uhh . . . Native, I think we're supposed to call them Aboriginals.

ROSE: Indigenous.

RALPH: Indigenous, YES! Indigenous. Uh . . . youth! Were innocently swimming they had a flat tire, they called in for help, and he took a gun and shot 'em. Ah . . . this-this was uh . . . y'know the message that was out there. And when uh the-they came up . . . to testify by this time uhh they . . . they were telling, spilling their guts, they were telling it EXACTLY what happened. And yet . . . it seemed like the next paper didn't cover any of this.

> *Three journalists:*
>
> JOSHUA, *forties, White.*
> TABITHA, *forties, White.*
> LENA, *thirties, White.*

JOSHUA: There's questions on how the media uh reported on all of this.

TABITHA: That's always bin the newspaper's job. Is te tell, te introduce are stories, tyue people tha' wouldn' nu—usually hear them.

LENA: I got feedback on both sides of it. I was told I was too sympathetic to Gerald Stanley, an' I was told I was too sympathetic to Colten Boushie.

TABITHA: People were accusing us of sending people to the GoFunMe page. Which, y'know, wasn' in are—wasn' are intention.

LENA: When Geral' Stanley gaw' onto the stand, tha' was the first time tha' we had heard his voice when his son got onto the stan' tha' was the first time we'd heard Geral' Stanley's fam'lee's side of tha' story. Uhm, but it's naw' because we didn' try, like I would say that I spen' MORE time trying to reach ow' to Geral' Stanley, and his lawyer, uhm than I did trying to reach ow to the Boushie fam'lee, an tha' was was just because of who made themselves available an' who didn't.

JOSHUA: I used te work uh other jobs, like in construction, and you can SEE at the end of the day so hopefully the good you did, right? You put a roof on someone's house. With journalism it's uh less quantifiable. At the end of the day uh it's very hard te know exactly what good you did or IF you did any good, right? Or if you stoked the flames of division, right? Uhh and so reporting on racism . . . always begs the question, are you exposing it and shining a light on something so that we can ca-name it and-and get rid of it uh ih by shaming it, OR are we giving voice to something abhorrent, right?

TABITHA: We consider areselves the paper of record, an' we-we ARE tha' like if you wanna know abou' the history of anything, you're going te look at are pages. An people will do that for history.

JOSHUA: If WE can as journalists uh reflect current events that are happening but contextualize it properly and teach people about our history then they can use that truth uh to . . . to make accurate decisions, have better more accurate rela—more accurate relationships right?

TABITHA: I have a, uh, wonderful guy who, uh Indigenous man who calls me? An' just talks to me about issues, and he told me, about a situation, right after the verdict where, uhm, some whi'e guys in a truck pulled up next to 'im an pretended to shoot 'im? An' so I wrote abou' that. An' I wrote aboud ih as a person who grew up in a rural area. I've never had my parents—anyone go after my parents, over anything I've wrih'en. Buh, absolutely that happened in the community that they lived in. After I dared te write tha'. They were just getting phone calls an', and uh, just like, how dare she just really, wanning them to be accoun'able an' communicating to them tha'-that I had become, uhm, like brainwashed or, like a city—how dare she, uhm, not present us as being . . . how dare she naw understand we deserve to be safe.

Rural Saskatchewan.

RALPH: It-it was a clash of culture, there's NO doubt about it. Why this-this trial has become uh . . . SUCH a FLASHpoint is because the Natives BEHAVED in SUUCH a-a boisterous fashion, in such a LOUD fashion of what theirr . . . reputation is. And in turn uh . . . the Gerald Stanleys portrayed their lifestyle very vividly, they were busy . . . working on a farm, the son came home from work—

Speaking at the same time:

(overlapping) And uhh . . .

ROSE: *(overlapping)* Minding their own business.

Minding their business, eh?

RALPH: Y'know he put his boots on and went to help his da—his uh parents to work, y'know. The work ethics there they-they minded their own business. So . . . this was such a DRAMATIC . . . CLASH of the White man's lifestyle compared to how the Native's have been behaving and what they were up to, all this time.

Scene 5—Sheldon

JUDGE, sixties, White.
CROWN, fifties, White.

JUDGE: Your next witness, Mr. Burge.

CROWN: Thank you, My Lord. Sheldon Stanley.

SHELDON, twenties, White.

Mr. Stanley, I understand when you and your father were working on the fence or the gate, something happened that caught your attention; is that correct?

SHELDON: Yes. As we-as we were getting ready to hang the gate, we could hear a-a vehicle coming down the road. It sounded like-it sounded like it had no muffler. And I mean, not-not out of place or anything, just loud and definitely got our attention. We kind of acknowledged it between each other and continued to work. So the-the vehicle then pulled up to the shop.

CROWN: Please continue and tell us what you saw.

SHELDON: We come up the hill towards the shop, you could hear the quad start. I started running, realizing that it wasn't somebody looking for parts, it was somebody trying to steal something. I had a tool belt on with a framing hammer from fencing. And I took that framing hammer and backhanded the front windshield of the car. I was mad. The car started to pull ahead. You could hear spinning gravel. I looked over. I could see my dad kicking the-the tail light of the car as it pulled away. Then as—once the car finally got going, we-we stopped and-and watched it, because it-it looked like it was leaving. It had a straight path out of-out of the yard. And when it got to about beside the—my mom's blue Ford Escape, it took a deliberate right turn through the rear-rear end of it.

CROWN: Okay. And then what happened—what did you do after that?

SHELDON: I took off running for the house. As I got up the stairs onto the deck, I could hear a gunshot behind me. Sound—it didn't sound like it was right behind me. It sounded behind me. As I went into the house, I could hear a second shot. Once I came out, I noticed that the rear passenger door of the car was open, the car that had entered the yard. There was—there was two girls huddled in the back seat behind the driver or behind the driver's seat. And as I came down the stairs, I could see my father walk up—walking up beside the-the vehicle that had come into the yard. And that's when I heard a third shot. I turned, and as my father walked around behind the back of the-the grey vehicle towards me with a-a gun in one hand and a magazine in the other. And he—he turned and looked at me like he was going to be sick, and he said, I-I don't know what happened, it-it just went off, I just wanted to scare them.

CROWN: Did he say anything else?

SHELDON: He said, I don't know what happened, I bumped him, and then it went off.

CROWN: Where was your mother?

SHELDON: After I saw them turn and go. I saw my mother at the-at the front of the vehicle, and she turned to me and said, Call 911.

CROWN: So what did you do?

SHELDON: I called 911.

CROWN: How many calls did you make to 911?

SHELDON: I think it was two or three. I lost the first 911 call. I was—went to call them back, I was walking back towards the-the power pole and the two vehicles, and that's when the-the two girls attacked my mom.

CROWN: Why don't you tell us what you noticed—all that you noticed about these two girls?

SHELDON: I noticed them huddled in the back seat. After I was on the 911 call, they got out of the vehicle. They were obviously upset, yelling at us and-and just-just yelling in general. They were pacing around the vehicle. At one point, they-they pulled the-the driver out of the vehicle.

CROWN: Out of what door?

SHELDON: The driver's door. They opened the door, and the-the driver kind of fell out. So his feet stayed in-in the vehicle, but his upper body and torso fell out onto the-onto the gravel. They then grabbed him and dragged him fully out of the vehicle. As they-as they pulled him out, that's when I-I saw the—what looked to be a barrel of a gun with no stock come out with-with the driver.

CROWN: Then what happened?

SHELDON: We go into the house. My mom makes a pot of coffee as we-as we wait because we were told help was on the way. And then we sat at the table in silence.

CROWN: You-you say you sat in silence, having coffee?

SHELDON: Yes.

CROWN: What do you mean?

SHELDON: Sat at the-at the dining room table in the house and had a cup of coffee.

CROWN: And who was with you?

SHELDON: Me, my mother, and my father.

CROWN: Okay. Was anybody talking?

SHELDON: No.

Scene 5.5—Coffee

Song: "Try to Understand."

HALEY, fifties, Indigenous.
Sparse music underscoring.

HALEY: The thing that bothered me the-the MOST out of this whole thing? It's when they made the statement that . . . while they were waiting for the RCMP . . . his wife had gone in and made coffee and they sat and drank coffee . . . while waiting for the RCMP. So you tell me how . . . I mean who sat with that boy? As a MOTHER! She has a child who's sitting with her. As a mother, there's a dead child in a vehicle . . . wouldn't ya cover him up or sit with him or hold their hand. Something until the RCMP got there. No you all go in and have coffee, and I would presume talk about who should say what . . . and because you're not just gonna sit there and have coffee after an incident like that you're gonna talk. I don't care what kinda family you come from. But for them to say that like the wife went in and made coffee and they went in and had coffee and waited for the RCMP, it's like . . . like just have . . . I dunno. Just no moral ca-connection I can't see a—leaving a child laying dead in a car. And you go in and have coffee. I mean . . . who does that?

Put on a pot of coffee
Help is on the way
Sit here in silence and try not to let your mind stray

Try to understand
A life was lost here on our land
Try to understand
The day didn't go as planned.

Scene 6—Streeters

BOBBY-JO (BJ), sixties, White.

BJ: My name is Bobby-Jo and I live in the City Park area.

GORDON and ALBERT, sixties, White.

GORDON: Uh we-we fix a lot of problems here at Starbucks, as soon as we walk away we forgot what we fixed. You gotta remember we're both seniors.

ALBERT: We're Starbucks buddies.

JOE and SUSAN are in their sixties, White.

JOE: Hi! I'm Joe from Lawson Heights.

SUSAN: I'm Susan from Lawson Heights.

BJ: Indigenous people have not really come that far.

ALBERT: I-I get frustrated with the fact that Indigenous people are still at the level they're at.

SUSAN: I think they're fine. We're all one people so as far as I'm concerned. I don't have anything against them.

JOE: Uh personally ninety-five percent are GREAT and the five percent are the ones everybody always remembers.

BJ: Y'know I've lots of Native friends who are EXTREEMELY well-educated. That is not what the general public see.

JOE: Down by the movie theatres hanging out on Twentieth Street there being a bit a—bit of a trouble.

ALBERT: I find it difficult not to uhm judge. Like I'm a pretty judgy person, I think. I think we're always judging . . . in life. We always judge. Our friendships, other people, other races, because we have preconceived notions of what . . . uh . . . what they're about, what they've gone through.

BJ: It makes me feel really sad. It makes me feel really sad. There are some people with mental health problems, there's a lo-lots of Indigenous people around, those people are not employable, they're not educated, they're not employable, and there's no place for them.

GORDON: Like downtown. Most Indigenous people you s-see or you notice they're beggin' for money. Well how do you not judge that? If all you ever see from the Indigenous people is somebody comin' on your yard trying to steal something. How are you s—NOT going to react to that?

JOE: Why are they held back? The Indigenous like—they start out in elementary school just like everybody else and they're great little kids and then by the time they reach grade nine/ten, that's when they're separated. Which is too bad.

BJ: I have family that live really nearby and it isn't cut and dried. I don't think that he purposely killed Boushie. I don't believe that for one minute. On the other hand, we cannot have people driving around with stolen liquor from a-a liquor board store they broke into which has never come out in public.

Scene 7—Crown Questions Youth

The CROWN *questions three young Indigenous people.*
They are at three separate witness stands.

JUDGE, sixties, White.
CROWN, fifties, White.

ERIC, twenties, Indigenous.
CASSIDY, eighteen, Indigenous.
BELINDA, twenties, Indigenous.

Song: "Try to Understand pt. Two."

CROWN: Mr. Meechance, I understand you are from the Red Pheasant First Nation?

ERIC: Yes, Your Honour.

Lighting shift.

CASSIDY: Cassidy Percy Phillip Cross-Whitstone.

CROWN: Do you remember that day?

CASSIDY: Bits and parts, yeah.

Lighting shift.

CROWN: Belinda Jackson.

JUDGE: Good morning, Ms. Jackson.

BELINDA: Good morning.

Lighting shift.

CROWN: Besides listening to music, was-was your group doing anything else?

Music underscoring comes in.

ERIC: They were drinking a little bit. But before that, we were just, like, shooting—like, targets or whatever with the—with our—with a .22.

CROWN: At-at Colten's grandmother's house?

ERIC: Yeah, just, like, in the backyard or whatever. And then from there, we-we went to—from his house, we went to Maymont through the back roads.

CROWN: At some point did you start to drink?

BELINDA: Yes. As we were leaving to—leaving the reserve.

CASSIDY: When we got to Maymont, we swam for a bit, maybe for, like, twenty minutes, half an hour.

ERIC: We turned around and we were coming back out, and then that's when we had got in a—we could just hear, like, a pssst. Like, got a heavily-a heavily—leak in a tire.

CASSIDY: I wasn't familiar with the roads, and they weren't really familiar because we were all pretty much out of it.

CROWN: Why-why were you out of it?

CASSIDY: Hammered. Drunk.

CROWN: Who was drinking?

CASSIDY: Everyone.

CROWN: How much did you have to drink, do you think?

CASSIDY: More than thirty shots.

BELINDA: Cassidy was-wasn't driving the way he was supposed to be. He was driving reckless. So as he was driving, like-like, we swerved off the road a little bit, and it caused our tire to pop off the rim. So we were riding on the rim for quite some time, I believe.

Driving and drinking, another summer day
Back road fun, just fading away
Holding my love, blinded to the world

CROWN: Did the location of people in the vehicle change, like where people were seated?

ERIC: Not really, besides Kiora climbing in front and sitting on Colten. And I was, like, teasing Colten because him and Kiora—I still laugh about this. Him and Kiora were, like, kissing real heavily there. I remember I grabbed them on their right shoulder, and I was, like, relax. I was, like, your nîstâw is right beside you. That means, like, brother-in-law in Cree, because Kiora and Cassidy are pretty much like brother and sister. And I was, like—I told them—I was, like, relax. I was, like, your nîstâw is right beside you.

CROWN: Carry on and tell us where you guys went.

ERIC: We kept driving—kept driving fast to try and make it as far as we could.

CASSIDY: We pulled into that yard. He seen a truck in a shed, and he said, Let's go check out that truck

ERIC: He checked that truck. And then he asked for something to—he wanted something hard to hit the window or whatever.

And then there was the—in the back, there was that .22, and then I grabbed that. And he used the stock end to try and get—bust the window.

CASSIDY: I tried smashing the window with it, but the gun ended up breaking. So I jumped back in the vehicle. And that's when I decided I was going to ask for help at the next farm because I didn't want to go any further.

CROWN: So where did you go next?

CASSIDY: We went to Gerald Stanley's farm.

Try to understand
A life was lost here on our land
Try to understand
The day didn't go as planned

BELINDA: I remember driving into the farm, and I remember seeing somebody on the right side of me, mowing their lawn.

CASSIDY: We went into the farmyard, I told Eric, I said, we're going to go—we're going to ask for help. He got out, and he jumped on that quad and he tried starting it.

ERIC: Cassidy jumped out, and then I jumped out after him. And then he, like, jumped on-on and off the quad. It didn't move one foot, like, not even half a foot.

CASSIDY: And then we heard yelling. And I panicked.

Music shifts.

I jumped in the driver's seat, and I started yelling at him. I was, like, what the hell are you doing? Get over here, what's wrong with you.

ERIC: And then, yeah, then we heard, like, Hey, what the fuck, or something like that, like, just, like, someone yelling.

CASSIDY: Before he could jump in, they were already pretty much at the vehicle. Gerald and his son.

BELINDA: Somebody smashed the windshield.

CASSIDY: All that glass came into my eyes, and it blinded me.

ERIC: There was a parked vehicle we hit it because the—we had it right on the rim on one side, and we weren't probably getting enough traction. And then—a big cloud of smoke from the radiator, then I just seen him open his door, the driver's side door, and he started running. And I opened my door and I took off running behind him.

CASSIDY: As I was running, I heard a ricochet, a bullet.

ERIC: I heard two shots. And I swear that those were towards me because you could hear, like, a whistling.

CASSIDY: It was, like, "ding," and it went up in the air. And then as I crossed the fence, I heard a bullet right beside my right ear. I panicked. I started running.

Shots rang out, glass everywhere
Running for my life, why did we go there?

BELINDA: So after they ran, I heard an old—like, a voice, saying, Go get a gun. And somebody went and—went in the house or somewhere to go get a gun.

CROWN: Tell us what you saw.

BELINDA: He came around the-the car, the vehicle, the passenger. And he shot Colten in the head.

CROWN: We have to go through these details, Ms. Jackson. So I'm sorry, but we have to do this.

BELINDA: I panicked and I woke up Kiora because she didn't—she didn't—she wasn't aware of that happening. I woke her up because I was screaming, and I told her what happened. And then she started reacting to it, and-and we didn't get out—none of us got out of the vehicle right away. And a while after, we-we managed to get out, and we got—we both got out of the vehicle. She opened the door, and he fell out of the—he fell out of the vehicle.

Body on the ground, no more sound
Arms are crossed, no mourn for the loss
Body on the ground, deafening sound
It all came down, it all came down

CROWN: And what happened after Colten fell out of the vehicle?

BELINDA: We kind of just stood around there, like, we just sat there, crying, for a while.

CROWN: What did you do?

BELINDA: I assaulted the-the lady there that was—I seen mowing her lawn.

CROWN: What did you do that was an assault?

BELINDA: Like, I punched her.

CROWN: Was she doing anything?

BELINDA: She was standing there with her arms crossed.

CROWN: And how many times did you punch her?

BELINDA: I don't really recall how many times I punched her, but I remember hitting her.

Try to understand,
A life was lost here on our land
Try to understand,
The day didn't go as planned.

CROWN: Please continue and tell us what happened.

ERIC: I started walking on the road, and I got to the bottom. And I was, like, halfways in between the hill. And then that's when that canine guy arrested me.

CROWN: Did you know what had happened to Colten at that time?

Music shifts to a slow tempo.

ERIC: No, that's—I found out in a pretty much, like, the worst way. I was in custody, and Belinda came in first. I remember-I remember everything because it was pretty-pretty hard the way I found out. We were in North Battleford cells, Belinda came in first, and she was, like, he's gone. And I was, like, what? He's—like, he's dead. I didn't, like, want to believe it.

Try to understand
A life was lost here on our land
Try to understand
The day didn't go as planned

Scene 8—Immigrants and Panhandlers

JULIA, thirties, White.

JULIA: Where I used to work we would employ a lot of recent immigrants from umm Sri Lanka or wherever uh, you know, uhh African countries, and they would come and they uh would be the blackest Black people. Within two weeks almost every immigrant can figure out the hierarchy of the races and that the Aboriginal people are the most despised people here.

FORBES, forties, Cameroonian.

FORBES: I was in Montreal working as a mailroom clerk. So when I told my boss that I was moving to Saskatoon for studies . . . the first thing he ask me was . . . how come you are moving to that city, where we have lots of Indigenous people?

MOHAMMED, thirties, Palestinian.

MOHAMMED: My community, the Arab community, they actual advise me, I have to live in the east side, not in the west side. Because the west side is there's a lot of homeless, a lot of . . . uhmm . . . y'know, not good people, living there, in the west side—most of the Indigenous people actually. Y'know, the First Nation Indians live in the west side. So if you wanna be safe, live in the EAST side, not in the west side.

DEVON, thirties, Jamaican.

DEVON: I see like the First Nations, they have a different perspective i—of livin' and you always see them lingerin' an wanderin'. Lingerin' an' wanderin' is meanin' like they-they all drugged out an' jus' lost and then you see them with dare kids jus' lost. Like don't have any hope, any at all in Saskatoon.

RICHARD, forties, Afghan.

RICHARD: My first impression with Indigenous people of course was—it was a disaster because you know, what I heard asss, y'know as a nyewcomer to Saskatoon, matching that with what I was seeing with my eyes, people were saying that these people are very lazy people.

HAJESH, twenties, Congolese.

HAJESH: I had never met Indigenous people. I din' know who Indigenous peoples were, so the first thing I was told about them was all-all the negative stereotypes you've heard ab—you've ever heard about them from are taxi driver, who's peeking us from thee airport, who's telling-telling my parents and my siblings an' I that they're drunkards, that they're single moms, that they waste their lives, that kinda thing, and like because I've never had contact with Indigenous peoples before, I thought that this was true.

DEVON: In my country an' in my culture or in Africa most people were in the same position and . . . some people arose from it and some people didn't. And I wonder if it was a thing from the womb where in . . . that-that slave mentality come down in the generation or something.

JULIA: Saskatoon is very divided and it's very divided along income level and unfortunately in our city income level are very—have a lot of connotations with skin colour. People's dislike of people in poverty is also confused with racism as well, or they're very interconnected.

DEVON: Immigrants, we come here under the circumstances of a hard life out in our country. And we come here to make ourself a little bit better dan to go lay down on de street ar te-te not be productive to the country.

JACK and PETE, forties, Indigenous.

JACK: Saskatoon's beautiful cun—I like it, I like the city. Like y'know some people that I meet, they, y'know, they are racist, but some people y'know, when I meet me here, we meet people every day. And they're nice to us every day.

PETE: Depends on what people you meet. Okay? Depends on what people you meet, okay?

CLARENCE, fifties, Indigenous.

CLARENCE: I usually eat at Friendship Inn or dig in the garbage eh y'know, for money y'know even chips or pop. Sandwiches. I'm down here downtown right now. I'm tryin te—I'm gonna try and do somethin'. Walk aroun' uhm . . . panhandle. *(laughs) Heh heh heh.*

PETE: But-but we-we're respect for each other as so that's how we are and that's how we ar ih—how we geew up.

JACK: That's how we're taught.

SAM, fifties, Indigenous.
SAM is walking by and interrupts the conversation.

SAM: *(interrupts)* Wanted you to hear it from a sober perspective, drug-free, alcohol-free.

CLARENCE: I found out my mom was dead.

A sixteen-second pause.

Yeah other than that uhm . . . doing good. Surviving every day. Yeah uh, my reserve is Thunderchild reserve an' . . . I don' wanna go over there. There's nothing for me over there. I lost my language.

I just—I'm tryin' to learn it back but it's hard. I'm Cree. I-I'm a Thunderchild. Thunderchild reserve.

SAM: It's always the street people speaking for our people. It portrays us wrong.

JACK: I like White people. I used to-I used to-I used to date White person.

PETE: (overlaps on last "I used to") —I like White people.

FELIX, forties, White.

FELIX: My son uh seven uh his best friend at school when he started there was Liam and I was like awesome have Liam over like awesome, Liam came to the door, Liam was an Aboriginal youth—kid seven-year-old and shouldn't make a snip of a difference but I can be totally honest and for a split second it kind of threw me, and it shouldn't have and I was like why did I—why did I get nervous with that?

WILL, thirties, White.

WILL: My family was one of those ones that y'know, Indigenous are bad, for the most part—there's a few good ones but overall in this province they're not good. I was one of those people that was my parents told me—taught me that, or my dad primarily, that y'know they're-they're almost not below us but like they're a lot of them are-are a problem.

ANNA, seventies, Indigenous.

ANNA: I must have been about probably in my mid-forties when I realized that I was one of the most racist people I knew. One day I-I heard myself saying something and I-and I stopped, I actually stopped what I was saying and I—it—and it felt like somebody was standing beside me saying it, you know. In my mind I felt like I wanted to look at that person and then I realized that-that I was saying that. And um I was really uh in shock. So is it possible that people don't know that they're—that racist or that they're-they're perpetuating that if I didn't until then?

PAMELA, fifties, Indigenous.

PAMELA: The normalizing of racism also comes from the people that are a part of are lives, that we interact with, y'know, are White grandmother, with her little white curly hair, who seems and who is, very sweet and kind and loving, but yet, has internalized these messages, that perhaps she hasn' created, but has become part of an understanding, of what is wrong in are society, but they just repeat those stories that they tell themself.

DANNY, thirties, White.

DANNY: We did do some awful things te-te the First Nations people. Butcha can't blame me. I'm a White guy and I didn't do that to them, right? And I have love for the Natives and y'know so you can't—like that was pretty gross and harsh and uncalled for and but it wasn't me.

VIHAAN, forties, Indo-Canadian.

VIHAAN: The billboards about privilege. I remember those billboards distinctly because we were driving along Circle Drive near the airport and . . . I was . . . annoyed by them. The message was, I the person looking at this was privileged and should check my privilege. It felt like an accusation. I don't deny immense privilege. But if someone says to me check your privilege it makes me think it's a challenge, it's an insult.

PETE: Us Native people, we're-we're pretty awesome te tell ya the tru—we're pretty cool guys and we have respect for everybody. But some-some White people, they think they don't have respect for ti—but we have respect for them.

CLARENCE: My heart it keeps me going. I don't harm anybody okay? We need the money so for something you know. That's why we ask but-but they don'—they don' give us anything but-but then they think we're assholes.

JACK: My dream is to come back teacher again. Yes, I really do. I have education.

PETE: Me, my dream-my dream is the same ah—I work at a farm. To me I work at a farm so I'm okay . . . Are you gonna pay me another five?

SAM: It's always the street people speaking for our people. Like you just uh spoke to a few people that they're kind-hearted people, loving people, but just by lookin' at them you can tell they're drinking. Some of us that don't drink SEE IT and we don't like it because it portrays us as people that don't have uh any other means but to drink. We're not all drunks and alcoholics.

"Picture on the Wall" music comes up, underscoring the final two lines of the scene.

DEVON: My-my question that I ask to dem is ih . . . do you have uh-uh desire for better life? Do dey have a dream?

SAM: We DO have a dream but lot of us don't know how to answer that question a lot of people probably don't know how. Same thing with when you ask a person uh why do you drink? They're pretty lost.

Scene 9—Immigrants

ANNA, *seventies, Indigenous.*
PHILLIP, *sixties, White.*
ROSE, *seventies, White.*

Song: "Picture on the Wall."

ANNA: Everybody was an immigrant at one time . . . y'know? Like your people didn't end up here because everything was great in the cu—in their in their homeland. Nobody leaves their homeland because . . . everything is wonderful. Most of the time they leave because they're . . . they're looking for a better place to raise their children, or they're running from war, or they're running from religious persecution, or whatever! I mean that's the history in Saskatchewan at least.

PHILLIP: I have-I have a picture in my above my wall of my grand-parents from uh . . . the Ukraine and my other ones who are from Eastern-Eastern Germany. They virtually didn't have an outhouse all through my dad's, all through their life on the FARM right? So they—are they the people the colonizers who came here and t-to-to wreck the land and to abuse and take advantage of everybody that was here? They came here living in-in sod huts, living in the side of-of-of uh hills—is was that what they expected to come to? No. That's the country existed at that time. Look at where the country is today. Everyone here today lives better than they did in 1920.

A picture on the wall that says it all
My grandfather standing so tall
See it in his face
His hands are worn from working the ground in this place
Broke his chains and carried on
To a better place where he belongs

ROSE: My uh . . . grandparents didn't expect anything from the government, they had to work on their OWN an-and I mean there was starvation, there was sicknesses and everything it wasn'—and they integrated into wherever they were eh? They took a lot of years, a lot a work, but they were determined, eh? Where I think . . . on the other hand there's always a gimme y'know? Like a gimme this gimme that, I want that. Where—but not TRYING hard enough f-for themselves eh? Uh . . . the Aboriginals eh, y'know?

**Mushom's picture on the wall
They tore him down and made him so small
You can see it on his face
Nowhere to go, no great escape**

ANNA: So those people across the street they don't care if their windows are popped outta their house and they got garbage laying all over or whatever which is what people always talk about. They don't understand about . . . what happens to people when they-when they've LOST everything and it's generations of that when there's-when there's nothing left, there's no hope, there's nothing. But people come here and they have a good life and they that-that's shut out that's not a part of their daily lives and then they look down on Native people and don't understand if you just pull yourself up by your bootstraps everything would be okay. But they don't realize that they had to leave their homeland in order to come and pull themselves up by their bootstraps and there were people there to help them to do that. And . . . we haven't immigrated. Y'know, we're here! And we're not going anyplace. But they don't SEE that as being maybe the same history as their great-grandparents'.

**What do you hang up on your wall
When your windows are broke and you've lost it all
Stuck in this place they filled with shame
They tripped you up and now they blame you for the fall**

Music out.

BRYAN, forties, White.
The following is spoken chorally, but BRYAN's surtitle remains.

BRYAN

(COLIN) One of the main reasons that people are better with, uh, people who are new to Canada than . . . the original inhabitants of this place is

(KRIS) if they are fleeing problems,

(TARA) or if they have struggles,

(COLIN) they're not struggles that challenge our world view of ourselves as

(ALL) good people.

(NATHAN) So if somebody comes fleeing Syria, and we help them

(KRYSTLE) we feel good about that.

(ALL) We didn't cause Syria.

(COLIN) Whereas, if people are living here,

(KRIS) and living here for generations,

(TARA) and they're struggling

(ALL) and suffering,

(COLIN) uh . . . we have to examine what our role is in that.

Scene 10—Complicated Truth

PHILLIP, *sixties, White.*

PHILLIP: I've worked in uh inner city for uh thirty years. Truth is complicated. We're not able to see the full picture and that creates a lot of disharmony with people when you only get half the story and you know there's another half there that they're choosing not to present.

Ever heard of Tomson Highway? So he speaks about he was taken to reserve to residential school from the age of one and he spent many years there and he has fond memories of that. And he talks about that's the only reason he was able to learn English, was able to learn to play the piano, and to have all the wonderful opportunities he had in the world, and that was— Because of residential schools that he was able to do that. Those were none of the stories that we got when we looked at the truth and reconciliation.

If the Boushies were not on that property, nothing would've happened. End of story. That's where that story started.

Thee young la' didn' deserve te die. 'Ers a lot of problems on reserves, with a lot a thee youths being addicted to different drugs or te alcohol. We get the opinion that they were just there that ONE day an' that was sorta thee, uhm, that they weren't INVOLVED in any other BAD events in their OWN communities an' other communities, and I don' know if that is true or not. I would like to know . . . the history of these youth—how they were seen by the rest of the people on the reserve before this event? Are these youth who y'know help Grandma across the street, and if they need a drive or groceries somewhere they go take her an' that. Are they youth who are addicted to different things and uh y'know you can't trust them that your car might be broken into. Who are these youth, right? Who are these youth?

Scene 11—Defence Questions Youth

The DEFENCE *questions the three Indigenous people.*

JUDGE, *sixties, White.*
DEFENCE, *fifties, White.*

ERIC, *twenties, Indigenous.*
CASSIDY, *eighteen, Indigenous.*
BELINDA, *twenties, Indigenous.*

Song: "Try to Understand pt. Three."

DEFENCE: Okay. Mr. Meechance, with somewhere between not drinking and blacked out, how many drinks do you think you had?

ERIC: Maybe, like, seven. Not, like, full cups or nothing. Just, like, swig of a bottle.

DEFENCE: Do you recall telling that officer—do you recall mentioning a gun at any point in that interview?

ERIC: No.

DEFENCE: Can you help me with that, why you wouldn't have mentioned anything about you guys driving around shooting out of the vehicle?

ERIC: Because I had a gun ban.

DEFENCE: Right. You've been convicted of-of a weapons offence yourself?

ERIC: Yes.

DEFENCE: And you have a five-year prohibition on using a gun?

ERIC: Yes.

DEFENCE: What does "checking vehicles" mean?

ERIC: I don't know. Like, just checking them, I guess. I don't know.

DEFENCE: Is this just a service that you're providing or is this—

ERIC: If that's what you want to say.

DEFENCE: What I want you to say is that you're looking at stealing things. Is that what was going on there?

ERIC: No. We didn't steal nothing. We didn't have nothing stolen in that vehicle. There was-there was nothing that was stolen in that vehicle. And it wasn't a stolen vehicle.

DEFENCE: What does "checking" entail?

ERIC: I said we—that vehicle was—the window was locked, and then he asked for something heavy, and I give it to him.

DEFENCE: Okay. So he tried to break into it?

ERIC: Yeah.

DEFENCE: Okay. So you gave him a loaded rifle?

ERIC: It wasn't loaded.

DEFENCE: How do you know it wasn't loaded?

ERIC: Because it—I don't think people would be driving around with a loaded gun.

DEFENCE: That would be crazy, to be driving around with a loaded gun?

ERIC: Yeah.

DEFENCE: To use a loaded gun to try to smash into a truck, that would be pretty reckless?

ERIC: Yes.

Lighting shift.

Try to understand
The choice was made before the tragic end
Try to understand
Who's to blame? Please take the stand

DEFENCE: So didn't you think the family deserved to know the truth about what was going on that day?

ERIC: What do you mean by that?

DEFENCE: Well, don't you think they deserved to know that you guys were out checking vehicles, that you had a-a gun in there, you were shooting a gun out of the vehicle, you were—drank a—what did you call it? A sixty-pounder?

ERIC: A sixty or forty, one of the two.

DEFENCE: So why would you go to the media?

ERIC: The family asked me to.

DEFENCE: The family asked you to?

ERIC: Yeah.

DEFENCE: Okay. Do you think that had anything to do with you leaving out the parts about checking the vehicles?

ERIC: Well, we were—are we here for that or are we here for—aren't we here today for Mr. Stanley?

Who's on trial here?
Can I get witness?
Let's talk about your past, boys
We can't dismiss this

Lighting shift.

DEFENCE: *(to CASSIDY)* So were you aware that all those lies were circulating in the media?

CASSIDY: What lies?

DEFENCE: Well, all the lies about you guys not stealing, not-not being armed?

CASSIDY: We didn't steal from Gerald Stanley's farm. We didn't—the media doesn't say that we didn't steal from those two other farms. We didn't steal nothing. What they said was we were looking for help when we went to Gerald Stanley's farm, and that is true.

DEFENCE: *(to ERIC)* So the media—there was a specific question whether you went to the Stanley farm to steal, and you said "no." Would you agree with me now that whatever was going on with the quad was not motivated by help for a tire, it was motivated by theft?

ERIC: But we did not take the quad.

DEFENCE: So you tried to take it, but it wouldn't go?

ERIC: What do you mean? Like—I just said we didn't take the quad. Like, the quad didn't move a foot.

DEFENCE: I think you're mixing up attempting to steal stuff and not actually getting away with it.

Try to understand
The choice was made before the tragic end
Try to understand
Who's to blame? Please take the stand

DEFENCE: You would agree with me that the suggestion that Gerry and Sheldon came out of nowhere, that that's not really fair? They were working, and you guys were stealing from them?

CASSIDY: No. I wasn't stealing.

DEFENCE: Sorry. Your group.

CASSIDY: Eric.

DEFENCE: Eric was stealing from them. So not-not unreasonable for Sheldon to run up and say—

CASSIDY: Yeah.

DEFENCE: —get the heck out of here?

CASSIDY: Yeah.

DEFENCE: Right. You'd be frustrated if it was your farm?

CASSIDY: M-hm. Well, yeah. Probably, yeah.

What would you do?
If they came to your farm?

And right away you knew
There was going to be harm

DEFENCE: You actually have a driving prohibition, right?

CASSIDY: I did.

DEFENCE: So you—your record includes—you had a fail-to-comply with an undertaking. And then we've got—flight while pursued by peace officer? And on that one, that's where you got the two-year driving prohibition.

CASSIDY: M-hm.

DEFENCE: At that same time, you have theft of motor vehicle.

CASSIDY: Yeah.

DEFENCE: Mischief under five thousand?

CASSIDY: Yes.

DEFENCE: Break-and-enter and commit?

CASSIDY: Yes.

DEFENCE: Theft—another theft of a motor vehicle?

CASSIDY: Yes.

DEFENCE: Another theft of a motor vehicle?

CASSIDY: Yes. I was just a kid. I still am.

Who's on trial here?
Can I get witness?

REASONABLE DOUBT | 47

Try to understand
The choice was made before the tragic end
Try to understand
Who's to blame?

Music out.

Scene 12—The System

PAMELA, fifties, Indigenous.

PAMELA: When I was listening to those kids' testimony, what really struck me was, in a way, how innocent they were. I mean, they weren't innocent, but they were, they were just so naive, in a way. It's almost like, you would think that they would know. How . . . harsh the system is gonna come down on them. An' they don' have a chance. THEY don' even get . . . how . . . discredited they are, as a people.

DENNIS, sixties, White.

DENNIS: Thirty some odd years of being a defence counsel for legal aid, I WILL SAY, and challenge anyone to dispute it, that the criminal justice system in Saskatchewan, is actually a machine SET UP to put Indigenous people in jail.

BARRY, fifties, Indigenous.

BARRY: I go to the correctional centre, and I see the people there, I go there to sorta teach Cree language. It's sad, because some a those people think it's their home. That's the justice system. Right? I mean it's not a justice system, it's a legal system.

PAMELA: Oh my god, these kids. They think that they can go out there . . . and play around, and be irresponsible . . . at the same level as White kids? Not on your LIFE.

DENNIS: We have this BULLY, in the room, that we're all too afraid te na-NAME, which is that institutional RAYcism . . . This ENSLAVES US ALL. This IGNORANCE . . . leaves us ALL . . . WEAK, an' COWardly, an'-an' fffilled with shame. That-that-that the aMAYzing potential that-that we have as a people is being deSTROYED, simply because there's a bully in the room, an' not enough of us are willing te take it on.

BRYAN, forties, White.

BRYAN: What would . . . what would balance look like, what would, uh, homeostasis, and uh, and uh, a positive relationship look like? How would you like me to be? How should White people be? How should . . . First Nations people be? How should, uh . . . new Canadians be in order to create, uh . . . balanced . . . healthy, fair, just society?

Scene 13—Questions

Rural Saskatchewan.

ROSE and RALPH, seventies, White.

RALPH: Here is what Colten Boushie posted on his Facebook page April 29:

The words are projected as RALPH speaks:

"Back in the saddle again, throw my middle finger up to the law. Ain't going to rob no one tonight. But to do it JUST because I'm a nut. I get bored, did some pills, but I want more. Fuck this world. Fuck this town."

ROSE: So-so he was miserable eh? He like . . . he didn't care.

RALPH: This was a snapshot.

Spoken quickly one after another without break:

Of his mind.

ROSE: His Life.

RALPH: At any given time.

ANNA, seventies, Indigenous.

ANNA: All of the people, in the courtroom were s—were the stereotype, and they played that. It was like the *(laughs) court was a* stage an' everybody was the actor an' they played out racist Saskatchewan. You know? Good for nothing Indians, racist redneck farmers. An' that's not what those people are. I know those farmers too. An' I know that they'd go out there and shoot somebody and- and that's scary an' I—and, but I also know that they're really good people. An' that they, that if anything happened, if my house were burning down they'd all be there te help me. But I've also heard them behave like that farmer an' talk like that. An' I've heard the same thing from Indigenous people. But nobody ever talks about that because nobody ever goes to that, to that place because maybe, maybe it's because we'd have to talk about things that we don't wan' to talk about. What we saw played out in the courtroom is exactly, what people know about Saskatchewan an'-an' about its people. An' that's not, that's really not who we are.

JUDGE, sixties, White.
DEFENCE, fifties, White.

JUDGE: Okay. Mr. Spencer, proceed when you're ready.

DEFENCE: Thank you. Thank you, My Lord. The next defence witness is Gerry Stanley.

End of Act One.

Act Two

Scene 1—Five Stories

There are five people standing at the front of the stage.

RONALD, sixties, Indigenous.

RONALD: There are many White allies who truly want to help, who are trying very hard to help. Got this thing called guilt in the way though, ummm I wish they'd get over it. Quit feeling guilty about what happened a hundred years ago and quit feeling guilty about residential schools and quit feeling guilty about everything that's happened to Aboriginal people and help us get through this mess that we're in now. I'd really like White people to quit telling victim stories, I'm tired of the social worker story that all of the problems with Aboriginal people come out of the fact that they're victims, quit telling victim stories about us, you're not helping. We're not victims, and the more you tell victim stories about us, the more you victimize us. If I tell you a placebo story, I give you a sugar pill and tell you this is good for you, that it's medicine, thirty-five to fifty percent of people will re—uh experience a reduction in symptoms. I give you the exact same sugar pill and tell you that this is poison, that it can kill you and make you very sick, you're probably going to get sick, and you could possibly die. It isn't the sugar in the pill that made him sick, and it's not the sugar in the pill that can kill you, it's the story. So if you're going to tell victim stories about us, know that you're killing us.

NOEL, *twenties, Indigenous.*

NOEL: I remember running. Doesn't matter why I was running. For an entirely legal purpose. And I remember running. And I remember a police car slamming on the breaks in front of me in an alley directly ahead of me and an angry White cop saying why are you running? And out of breath I could only muster four words. *Snakes on a Plane.* Because the matinee started in ten minutes. He has a gun. He has another one in his car. He has EXPERIENCE with Indigenous people . . . And when you deal with it on a daily basis, you start to look for the thing you're looking for and you start to SEE the things that you're looking for. And if you're a hammer everything looks like a nail.

ANGEL, *thirties, Indigenous.*

ANGEL: I live in Saskahood no I'm kidding, I live in Pleasant Hill uh my name is Angel and uhm yeah I'm a resident here *(laughs) heh heh heh heh heh heh heh.* I've lived in Saskatoon off and on for eight years going on eight years in January. Saskatoon is a place for me for growing and opportunity and also it's a place for . . . learning on both sides of injustice and justice relationship . . . The first time we got introduced to gangs I must've been like about maybe twelve or thirteen. I can't remember. Yeah, and uhm what my bro—my big brother introduced us and he said because our family was split up he said uhm this is our family.

NOEL: My mother is uh White uh she is uh descendant from farmers that came from Norway. Uh my father's First Nations he's descendant from First Nations people uhm who grew up on these lands an' uh she was raised down south he was raised up north, they met in the middle in Saskatoon and had me and I'm—I am uh a product of that willingness to see beyond what is normative and pervasive in the discourse. And so I got to go to uh . . . east-side schools, I got to have a White mother pick me up, I got to have uhm that privilege of her protection of being normative! And that made me in turn believe I was normative uhm until I was exposed to that racism uh that's so pervasive and that continues to be pervasive.

ANNA, *seventies, Indigenous.*

ANNA: This is a racist country. Every single day, kids are facing racism. I have great-grandchildren that are in school. Some of them look really Indigenous, some a them are Black children, an' they-they-they face racism from all a those places. But there are other things *(laughs) huh,* the—y'know that's just, when we talk about layers of stories, that's just one layer. You know it seems like we can't get past that place. An' I-an' I—maybe it's my age but I just—I-I wanna get PAST this. Uh—I wanna be able te find out why, why can' we have a conversation. Y'know? Why can' we have a conversation even among ourselves. It's just the one song. Why do we have so much trouble writing a new song?

NOEL: Race relations in Saskatoon are . . . polite uhm but insincere. People don't want te be seen as being racist but they often don't go out of their way to learn about uh . . . the misconceptions the-the-the preconceived notions of who and what we are and what we do uhm . . . but everyone's nice. Everyone uh seems to smile. And especially with me with a White voice and very hipster looking prescription glasses I feel I'm safe in that I'm wrapped in privilege, but at night when people don't get te talk to me and all they see is my resting stoic Indian face dressed in all black, they clutch their bags a little tighter, they move over to the sidewalk a little more.

RONALD: My name is Ronald Taylor. I'm a trapper, commercial fisherman. I have twelve sleigh dogs and I live at the north end of Montreal Lake on the land that my grandfather took after the Indian people were kicked out of Prince Albert National Park in 1928. We create this idea that there are different people on the planet. The only thing that holds me together with my race, if I belong to one as an Aboriginal person from this territory, is the stories that we tell ourselves. I am genetically almost identical to everybody else on this planet. There's very, very little genetic difference between me and kiciwamanawak we are humans first. Race is a story that we tell ourselves about ourselves. It doesn't exist anywhere other than in the stories that we make up, tell ourselves, tell each other, and the stories are not true.

ALICE, teens, *Indigenous.*

ALICE: On the bus, I 'unno, I was just, I was shivering, and there's this woman, like, sitting across from me, and she's wearing a hic—niqāb, and then she just came up to me, and checked my temperature, and she said something in her own language, and then shaked my jacket. *(laughs) Heh,* it just felt, I dunno, it's like, it's like she cared if I was warm or if I was cold. I dunno. It's just different, 'cause I don't even know her, and then there's a lot of other race, like, I experience racism, but then I never experienced anything like that before.

ANGEL: The streets of Saskatoon are *(exhale) hhh* violent and non-violent they're worthy and unworthy. It's depending where you walk and how you look at the streets. Uhm there are a lot of people that are caring and there are a lot of people that are in death. So sometimes there's no reality on the streets but when you're healthy there's reality of living a life that you could be successful in. And that you could walk down the streets without having somebody trying to look at you or buy you when you're not for sale.

ALICE: Someone who doesn't know how to speak my language or someone who doesn't know me . . . someone who I've never met before trying to . . . tell me that they're worried that I'm wearing a thin jacket in the winter. Like . . . like why didn't my family tell me that? *(laughs) Heh heh,* just kidding. But for real, she showed me that . . . just by showing you care a little bit can affect someone's decision on . . . teaches someone how to care for themselves.

ANGEL: Gangs is sisterly and brotherly love, that's all you get you don't get a parent out of it. It gave you a sense of belonging, it gave you an identity when you don't grow up with—when you haven't grown up with your culture or identity or anything of who you are, and when you're come from a family that split up and y'know you get teased for the colour of your skin, being in a gang gave you a sense of iden-identity and it gave you self-worth a-a respect.

ALICE: I grew up in, uh, Witchekan Lake First Nations, that's up north. Whenever we go to a house, we weren't afraid to, like, just— make ourselves a plate of food, because, like, um, I dunno, like . . . we just, um, invite people, and they just come eat at our house, so we just, um, watch TV or just, sometimes, the family would all just get together, and we're all just chillin' in a house, talking.

I think it was about . . . grade . . . five, um . . . there was . . . I notice that people were, um, like doing . . . doing drugs around there. And, yeah, and they like . . . and the older grade, like, grade seven people were . . . were already, um, getting high and stuff. I feel like the need to do it with them, and like I—like, I wanna party too, and do stuff like that because there's like people at my age that are drinking also, and, like, getting pregnant, and then . . . Um . . . My, my kokum found out and she just looked at me differently. She talked to me differently, like, I didn't know any better. I wanted to . . . go back to way it was before when people . . . had respect for me because, when you do drugs you're kinda looked down on everywhere, and you kinda just get used to that feeling.

ANGEL: I was just another statistic of being a single mother on welfare, drunk and y'know kids in-n-out of the system and y'know another—never a mother that was stable or being able to uh provide for my children coming out of the gang lifestyle because that was my identity at the time and that was my reality that was my safe place and nobody can bother me or touch me because I was the centre of the universe an' on the streets. In reality like MY reality my gang reality.

Song: "Everything Beautiful Takes Time."

Music underscoring comes in.

ALICE: We're like, brought up to live a religious life, and I liked it because I love dancing. And I was, uh, I was a princess, for our, um . . . reserve. And I, um, represented at Witchekan, and other, um . . . powwows. I made a vow when I was princess, that I said that I wouldn't—I wouldn't do drugs for a year, so I could dance again. But then I tried drugs, and then, I don't wanna . . . I don't wanna engage in them anymore because I wanna dance again.

I want to dance again
It feels right
I took a wrong turn somewhere
In my life

ALICE: My regalia has a spirit with it. 'Cause when I dance, and I put it on I feel more . . . more connected to my ancestors, I sus—I don't know. I just feel like, I feel like, um, someone higher.

Everything that's beautiful
Everything that's beautiful
Everything that's beautiful . . . Takes time

ALICE: Everything beautiful always takes time. And, when, um . . . everyone's just around, and, like, you can just feel the vibe of people getting ready for grand entry. Just, like, someone . . . braiding hair, and then putting on regalia, putting, um, beaded stuff on your hair. And I just feel real pretty when I'm in my regalia too. And then everyone's lookin' at you. Like . . . and then you're just making your family proud by dancing also.

'Cause when they call your name
You know you're still the same
Like a fractured windowpane

The light finds a way
When we look at you
You feel the truth
When you look at them
We feel it too

Everything that's beautiful
Everything that's beautiful
Everything that's beautiful . . . Takes time

The music trails off under the next speech.

RONALD: I drank quite a bit when I was in the navy, as a proper sailor should. You know, a lot of rum, a lot of foreign ports. I worked mining and logging and you know, there's some serious drinking takes place in the mining camps, frontier-style drinking in the mining towns across northern Western Canada. Then I went to university aaand my drinking changed and I was drinking twelve-year-old Scotch because that's the story I was telling myself. Expensive twelve-year-old Scotch because that was a class drink— that's the drink that judges and lawyers, people like that drink right? But then I wasn't doing that aery much anyway and I was down to about a glass every six months aand one day I went into a bar here in Saskatoon aand ordered a glass of single malt twelve-year-old, aaand they gave it to me and I tasted it and it tasted like shit. And I realized I'd been lying to myself, I'd been lying to myself telling myself that this shhhhit tastes good. And of course everybody knows it tastes like shit 'cause the first time you tasted it it tasted like shit and you had to lie to yourself for a long time before you could convince yourself that this shhhit tasted good. And when I realized that it still—realized again that it tasted like shit, well why did I waste good money on this stuff?

I am challenging the alcohol story. Five, ten years ago it would be very hard to have a conversation about alcohol. White people were scared to talk about it because if you said Indians and alcohol in the same sentence people would point at you and call you racist and nobody wanted to say anything. Indians were afraid to say Indian and alcohol in the same sentence 'cause they were scared White people would point at them and call them lazy dirty drunken Indians. So nobody talked about it. More recently, people are willing to start talking about it. 'Cause we've had enough now. Enough. We've buried enough. There've been enough deaths, too many missing sisters.

ANNA: I was raped by three RCMP when I was thirteen . . . in-in an' after one afternoon when my-my dad was gone an-an uh y'know, I was home alone with little kids. It was about race . . . because they talked about, the way they talked an'-an' that's when I knew that . . . 'cause it was my first time that I ever really had an ugly encounter with-with people like that.

I mean it's such a long time ago but it's but what I'm saying is that when-when that happened to me it was . . . it was like I was looking at it? I always remember that the-the first one, remember the look in his eyes, y'know. And that's the look I see in-in-in eyes of-of-of people that are . . . that I find really frightening, an' Stanley's one of them, Nerland was another one. Y'know? Uh, just this . . . i-it's I dunno what-what to call it. It's like a there's no conscience there. It's . . . it's something that's empty. An'-an' really uh . . . lots of HATE. Y'know, I was more overwhelmed by the hate than I was by the actual . . . by the actual rape.

MARY, forties, Indigenous.

MARY: That very evening that Colten was killed, the RCMP barged into Debbie Baptiste's trailer, that's Colten's mom. An' asked her something te the words, Who is Colten Boushie te you? An' when she answered, my son, she was callously told, oh he's deceased. She fell on the floor crying. The RCMP then proceeded te search 'er house. She told them that she was waiting for Colten. That his dinner was sitting in the microwave. That he couldn' be dead.

So they went an' they checked the microwave, te see if his dinner indeed was in there, an' it was. They then smelled her breath, 'n' asked her if she had bin drinking. They exited immediately, 'n' left Debbie like that, devastated, without support. His family, still, they hoped for justice.

DENNY, fifties, Indigenous.

DENNY: Why did you do it? Why did you kill Colten?

A five second pause.

Is it because you have so much hatred in your heart? You killed an innocent young man . . . a young man that had so much potential to live life, enjoy life . . . te have a family, te have kids, te have a wife. You took that away from him! He meant a lot to us. He was like a son to me. This kid never did anything to you, wouldn't have done any harm. You killed him! An innocent kid! Is why I hi—I fight so hard! So my nephew can get justice! This heartache, this hurtness, it HURTS!

Scene 2—Rural Reality A

Rural Saskatchewan.

BILL, sixties, White.
KEN, fifties, White.

Song: "We Had Hope."

BILL: I've lived in this town uh since I was born here, *(inhales)* raised on a farm, north a here.

KEN: Born an' raised, on the farm, an' have a family. Life's good. You know everybody and everybody knows you. You don't have to signal because everybody knows where yer goin. *(laughs)* Heh heh heh heh heh heh. And it's a great place to live and raise a family.

BILL: These days it's not quite the same, there's bin a, a bigger influx of uh people, an' at one time in my life, I would've known ninedy-five plus percent of the people. An' today it is probbly closer in the fifty percent range of people IN and surrounding area.

KEN: A long time ago the oil field wasn' there an' it was nice, 'n' now it's ge'in' busier 'n' busier, ann' I kinda wish it would be back to the old ways. Y'knew everybody that was drivin' down the roads 'n' now ye don' know who's who. So yer always on guard.

BILL: It's a little different than a person in the city where . . . when you lock yer door, you feel safe, an' that's the way you should feel, because that is yer home. For us on the farm, it's more like when you drive in yer yard, that's yer yard.

KEN: Yer safe haven.

BILL: I've always felt this but, are rural land gets no respect. An' I donno what kinda person Gerald is, but, when you've had somebody breakin' in an' stealin stuff outta yer yard annn', y'know. I can see it, where ye don' feel safe, you don' feel comfortable an'—

KEN: It would wear on a person.

Music underscoring comes in.

BILL: The situation inn the country is a lot different than in the city, an' not that it's more dangerous, but response time of anybody te help ye is significantly different. In the city at least you know that they're gonna be there in four or five minutes. In the country it could be three of four hours.

There'd beee nno chance, if somebody drove in the-in the yard an' was lookin fer help or had a flat tire, or, anything, that you'd ever have a gun an' come, y'know, standin' by the door, an' who's out there? What's goin' on? Mind you then, the other case is if somebody was there, stealin' gas outta yer yard or breakin' inte the shop, you might come te the door, an' then you think yeah maybe I'm goin' back down, I'll go downstairs an' grab the shotgun an'—

KEN: Well that'd be the last thing I'd think of—

BILL: You might not—

KEN: —is grabbing a gun.

I wouldn't. I would just—what are ye doin', y'know? Y'know. I feel safe. *(laughs) Ha ha ha ha, I gotta* . . . I dunno. I just, I'm comfortable out there. And so are my family. They're all comfortable.

BILL: I th-I think the reason that you feel safe, is because nothing's ever happened to us.

KEN: Good point.

Born and raised
Country and the city ain't the same
A lot of different faces, they don't wave
But we still feel safe

Scene 3—Stanley Testifies A

The DEFENCE and CROWN examine STANLEY.

> CROWN, *fifties, White.*
> DEFENCE, *fifties, White.*
> STANLEY, *fifties, White.*

DEFENCE: The next defence witness is Gerry Stanley.

What's your occupation, Gerry?

STANLEY: I'm a rancher and a truck driver and a part-time mechanic.

DEFENCE: Tell me about part-time mechanic.

STANLEY: Well, mostly people in the community. I fix vehicles.

DEFENCE: Do you ever help people off the road?

STANLEY: Oh, yeah.

DEFENCE: Do you have tires in stock?

STANLEY: I have used tires from—I don't know where they all came from, but—

DEFENCE: So you'd be able to probably get somebody back on the road?

STANLEY: Oh, yeah.

A lighting shift.

CROWN: Mr. Stanley, you had a lot of guns in your house; is that correct?

STANLEY: There was a few, yes.

CROWN: How many?

STANLEY: Hmm. Well, I'm not sure how many. I know how many worked, I can tell you.

CROWN: How many worked?

STANLEY: About five.

CROWN: You—did you ever get a hunting licence?

STANLEY: Yes.

CROWN: And you have a licence to hold restricted firearms?

STANLEY: Yes.

CROWN: In either of those processes, did you have to go through any firearms safety programs?

STANLEY: Yes.

CROWN: Tell us what you learned in the firearms safety programs.

STANLEY: Well, they tell you the actions of your firearm and safety aspects of it.

A lighting shift.

DEFENCE: So August 9th, 2016, can you tell me—tell me about that day, Gerry?

STANLEY: Well, I did what I do every day. I got up and had a couple cups of coffee and then went outside to start the day.

Start the day
Couple cups of coffee
And you're on your way
Watch another day go through the door
Everything in my life stays the same

Music out.

Scene 4—Aftermath

BERT, fifties, Indigenous.

BERT: The positions were polar within . . . twelve hours. First Nations community was absolutely uh . . . CERTAIN without knowing everything that this was a racist incident. The White community was absolutely CERTAIN that Stanley was defending his property. And once those voices were up and yellin', nobody was listenin'. Nobody was listenin'.

The racist comments started coming right away, both sides, right? It was-it was, the vehemence was AMAZING, it was AMAZING. And it was—it really showed uh y'know that . . . a-at-at some level those relationships are fragile . . . if our leaders let them be.

Scene 5—Rural Reality B

Rural Saskatchewan.

BILL, sixties, White.
KEN, fifties, White.

BILL: It's a problem, of people, not of specific race or creed. I don' care who they are . . . if they were White Black Pink er Yellow that arrs—tryin' te steal yer stuff, not a reason te shoot 'em. But ye feel—ye feel when they're threatenin' yer property—ye feel almost personally threatened.

Music underscoring comes in.

KEN: I-I'm gonna protect my stuff. I'm gonna protect my family. I mean, if there's trouble yeah, I'm gonna f—protect them. But I don' think I could pull the trigger but . . .

BILL: If I was in 'is boots that day . . . I would've approached 'imm similar way of—y'know, once they started, uh, aggressively tryna start stuff, bang inte stuff, then I woulda bin aggressively holler- ing an, y'know get the hell outta here whatever type a thing. Annd . . . ah, I'm a little differen' than Ken if it—if they were threatening my family or if I thought they were, I could easily, I think I could brandish a gun er whatever it took to, uhm, y'know, te try an' have enough force te get em te get the hell outta the yard. Annd . . . *(clicks tongue)*

KEN: Well I'm callin' the cops that's fer sure.

BILL: Oh that'd be—

KEN: That'd be number—

BILL: One.

But if my wife was out there an' it—she looked in danger, if push came te shove . . . I would defend myself te—and my family te the- the end. It's just . . . the feeling I have in my heart.

I hope that 'ee . . . didn' shoot the kid intentionally. I hope it was an accident. I hope becaussse I honestly feel fer the—y'know like young Col'en. I respect human life, uh, think it's hugely va— impor'ant . . . I love, my farm, I love farming, I LOVE this town, I LOVE this province, and I love this country. I just wish people would appreciate what they have annd uh, respect what everybody else has.

Scene 6—Stanley Testifies B

CROWN questions STANLEY.

CROWN, fifties, White.
STANLEY, fifties, White.

CROWN: What care were you taking with this handgun to make sure it didn't discharge at this person in the front seat? Were you taking any care?

STANLEY: Well, in my mind, it was empty, so I was just holding it.

CROWN: Do you-do you agree that the gun would have been pointed directly at his head—

STANLEY: No.

CROWN: —when it-when it—the gun would have been lined up right at his head—

STANLEY: No.

CROWN: —when it discharged?

STANLEY: I couldn't say that.

CROWN: How close were you to him? Close enough that he could touch you?

STANLEY: Yeah.

CROWN: You could—you tell us you could grab the keys with your left hand, reaching through the driver's window?

STANLEY: Yeah. I had to reach in.

CROWN: Well, you had-you had to reach as far as the steering column?

STANLEY: M-hm, and beyond. So . . .

CROWN: And you had a gun in your right hand?

STANLEY: Yeah.

CROWN: Why did you have your gun, this gun, inside that cabin of that vehicle?

STANLEY: Well, I didn't even realize I did have it inside.

CROWN: Well, it's-it's a gun. Don't you-don't you—

STANLEY: When it's empty, it's just a piece of metal, you know—

CROWN: When it's empty—

STANLEY: —which I thought—

CROWN: —it doesn't blow somebody in the head?

STANLEY: That's right.

CROWN: What are you suggesting, then?

STANLEY: I don't know what the—I was doing with the right hand.

CROWN: Pardon me?

STANLEY: I don't know what the right hand was doing.

CROWN: Well, it's your right hand.

STANLEY: Yeah, well, I wasn't looking at it.

CROWN: With a gun in it?

STANLEY: Right.

CROWN: With somebody right in front of you?

STANLEY: Yes.

If you can't hunt with a handgun
Then what is it for?
Thank you, Mr. Stanley
We don't need any more
You didn't know what your right hand was doing
Happens all the time

Music out.

Scene 7—Tragedy

ANNA, seventies, Indigenous.

ANNA: I turned the-the news on and they-they were just talking about it an' I burst into tears. Like you KNEEW that he was gonna get acquitted. Most of us knew that. Or at least those of us who have been around for a while. You know it's going to get worse. It's going to get worse.

ANGEL, thirties, Indigenous.

ANGEL: All I heard when Colten Boushie got uh murdered was a White man shot him in the back of the head. That's all that stayed. I didn't look at anything else. I just thought of a murderer. And he's gonna get away with it, which he did. Because he is White.

And that he would have like, because he's a farmer, he provides for Saskatchewan.

RONALD, *sixties, Indigenous.*

RONALD: Race relations in Saskatchewan uh hhh—is about fear. We're afraid of each other. The Gerald Stanley trial, way it ended was complete, and the verdict came down uh I shut off the radio, I shut off social media, and the next day I was on my way to a ceremony. And we're travelling through southern Saskatchewan aand . . . my wife says pull over somewhere but not in a farmyard. And I realized she was afraid. Aand my wife's not afraid of anything. This is a woman who walks in the wintertime when there's wolves around annd . . . nothing scares her. And then I recognize that the reeason we're afraid of the farmers is because the farmers are afraid. So we're all afraid of each other. Annd we don't talk.

WILLIAM, *sixties, White.*

WILLIAM: If Gerald Stanley if you see 'im as a one-dimensional, youuu could dismiss that an' say oh he—y'know, Gerald Stanley's a bad man, or-or at the very least he made a terrible mistake. But it doesn' bring out the *(laughs)* dis*comfort* that says . . . could I be capable of that? For ME, it makes me look at that dark side that I, personally, would rather not have to look at.

PHILLIP, *sixties, White.*

PHILLIP: I was at White Buffalo when the Elder, who I have great respect for, he started that circle with . . . there were two f—there was tragedy in two families. The Stanley's and the Boushie's. He says let's have a prayer for both families 'cause both families were-were-were faced trauma because of this event. And then it went around the circle. And that thought was lost. It was just one-sided. There was only one guilty party.

Scene 8—Closing Arguments

The DEFENCE and CROWN give their closing arguments.

JUDGE, sixties, White.
DEFENCE, fifties, White.
CROWN, fifties, White.

"Reasonable Doubt" music underscores.

DEFENCE: This whole situation is bad and sad, so sad. That is not lost on-on any of us. What do we know for sure?

CROWN: I'd like to address the things that we know for sure.

DEFENCE: The group of young people were not just going home from a day of swimming at the river on a hot day. They were up to no good.

CROWN: We know that this Tokarev handgun, the trigger has to be pulled each time that the gun is fired. It requires a distinct pull each time.

DEFENCE: What really matters is what the Stanleys experienced, what Gerry experienced, what led up to the tragic accident. Put yourself in Gerry's boots.

CROWN: Was it pulled intentionally? Was it—did it go off accidentally?

DEFENCE: I live in the city, I've got the luxury of calling 911. Gerry didn't have that luxury.

CROWN: If it went off accidentally, look at all the other circumstances and look how Gerald Stanley handled this firearm.

DEFENCE: The gun goes off. Freak accident.

CROWN: Gerald Stanley took no precautions and was exceedingly reckless.

DEFENCE: Was he reasonable? Was he-or was it a marked departure from what you'd expect of the average person, a marked departure from how you might have reacted in those circumstances?

Scene 9—Why?

Music shifts.

PHILLIP, sixties, White.

PHILLIP: Why the incident happened? I think what we have is ... things just build up and build up and then all of a sudden an event happens. And it's like a spark, could be spark for discussion. Unfortunately, it becomes a spark for people to pull away and-and just off the bat, take their own viewpoint and not take the whole look at the picture.

Scene 10—Judge's Charge

The JUDGE charges the jury.

JUDGE, sixties, White.

Song: "Reasonable Doubt."

JUDGE: It is your duty to decide whether the Crown has proved Gerald Stanley's guilt beyond a reasonable doubt.

Did Gerald Stanley cause the death of Colten Boushie unlawfully by committing an assault? Did Gerald Stanley have the state of mind required for murder? Did Gerald Stanley cause the death of Colten Boushie unlawfully by careless use of a firearm?

Shots rang out
It all came down
The choices made
Whose to blame?
Put on a pot of coffee
And sit in silence
Bodied in the driveway
Anyone would have done the same

Hey, wait, hey, wait
There's reasonable doubt
Hey, wait, hey
There's reasonable doubt

Some days don't go as planned
You lose your right hand
The bullets hanging there
Was only meant to scare
There's magic in the air
Nobody to blame
You would have done the same
Is this the only way?

Hey, wait, hey, wait
There's reasonable doubt
Hey, wait, hey
There's reasonable doubt

Was it unlawful?
Was there a trigger pull?
Was this a bad day?
Are we caught in old hate?
A spark and then a flame

Maybe we are all to blame
Things change but still the same
Reasonable doubt

Scene 11—What Now?

NOEL, twenties, Indigenous.

NOEL: Bullets. The sound. The . . . the imagined feeling of knowing that is . . . something that a human could feel. Every major pop, I wonder, did I feel anything above my ear.

ALICE, teens, Indigenous.

ALICE: It makes me feel scared— It felt like all White people are bad . . . all White people want to shoot us.

NOEL: I feel like we have . . . ways to go. To come to a place socially where we as a collective uhm hold our hearts when a situation like that happens instead of celebrating uh the protection of an ATV.

ALICE: I just thought it was wrong that someone got shot . . . in the head while they were sleeping. How could you accidentally shoot someone in the head? That's crazy.

NOEL: Twelve people on a Saskatchewan jury chose to believe in a theory of a magic bullet than racism.

JEFF, sixties, White.

JEFF: That's an understandable sentiment for somebody who PERHAPS hasn't taken the time te understand the way the jury system works. It must be beyond a REASONABLE doubt. The magic bullet that's a catchy expression but there's a crimp in that brass that was made somehow and when the bullet comes out and lands on thee uhm . . . on the dashboard of the vehicle so HOW does a bullet fired from a gun actually have a crimping and a folding on the case?

ANNA: It's ALWAYS been about race. It's been about race for . . . a loong long time. I can't even imagine when it wasn't about race. Then there's sometimes like in cycles where it's worse than-than it is other times. But it's always been about race. There's nobody that'll ever convince me it's not about race.

MACK, sixties, Indigenous.

MACK: The trial for the, Gerald Stanley for the killing of Col-Colten Boushie was a defining event for this province. It brought the use of racism to stark reality and in the END . . . the province of Saskatchewan was the one on trial. Stanley may have walked free, but the province was found guilty.

Scene 12—Change

TASHA, forties, White.
She is driving on patrol.

TASHA: Back in the early days a call related to like a stabbing or uh even having knives involved . . . uh was just rare. But I would say it seems like on average every set of four-day block we're working we're dealing with stabbings and calls related to knife violence. Firearms. Absolutely! Anecdotally the numbers have just skyrocketed, and the part that's bothersome to me is it's kinda becoming the new norm and I worry that if we don't do something quick to address the level of violence that's occurring on the streets it's just gonna become, how we operate, you know?

ANGEL, thirties, Indigenous.

ANGEL: This one moment I came home from work. All my like my-my gang brothers were there. And—my children were downstairs they stayed in this one room where nobody was allowed to go in because the kids were there because y'know there was dope upstairs there was weapons upstairs. And I came home an' I went downstairs inte my uhm rumpus room an' there was a guy, he was laying on my couch and he was literally beaten to a point where he looked like death an' I seen him laying on the couch.

TASHA: There's just so many young people in my division where you have conversations with them like . . . What do you wanna be when you grow up? Like . . . What are your big goals an' dreams for the next year or two? An' there's just such a sense of loss of purpose and loss of hopefulness and I just . . . I dunno like how can we start I guess at the kid level an'-an' bring back like . . . worthiness and purpose.

ANGEL: Two days had passed and I asked about him and they said that he died. And that uh don't worry about it two bros went to his funeral. And I thought what—that doesn't—I was like is this what my children are gonna go through when they get their minute? Like that's what I really thought. An' like are they gonna get this beat up where they gonna have to die two days later like this guy died? And so at that point in time I knew that I had to . . . search and find my way out because I didn't want my children to die.

TASHA: I was driving down back alleys and it happened to be Mother's Day and I stopped at a particularly . . . disastrous back-yard, garbage . . . STREWN all over the alley and in the yard and broken down cars, broken down furniture, and a kid sitting on the back stoop with his head in his hands. I would guess he's about twelve, maybe thirteen years old.

So I parked my car and got out to have a visit with him an' said, Well, it's Mother's Day, why don't you do something nice for your mom today and he just said my mom's passed out on the couch, she has addictions, I might as well not have a mom. And he got kinda teary-eyed and it-it just seems like it's that story's repeated and repeated an' I said well I'm a mom and it's Mother's Day so how 'bout for-for me you pick up all the trash in the backyard and throw it in that bin and I'll come back tomorrow night and if you do an awesome job I'll take you for treats. And he kinda lit up and he just like seemed to enjoy the engagement. The next night I went by the back alley and he was sitting there with probably twelve of his friends and when he saw my patrol car he JUMPED up with this huge smile on his face and came running towards my car saying I knew you'd come, they said you wouldn't come, I knew you'd come.

RONALD, sixties, Indigenous.

Music underscoring.

RONALD: We have to remember what the treaties were. When Alexander Morris came out here to negotiate the number of treaties, he used words like, "As long as the sun shines, the grass grows and the river flows." He talked about "Our mother, the Queen," he talked about brother to brother relationship. If you're a Cree, sitting on the ground, on Mother Earth, on your mother, getting her strength in these negotiations and you're listening to this, and you saw Alexander Morris smoke a sacred pipe at the beginning of the negotiations, if you looked at your own culture, you would see this treaty making ceremony as an adoption ceremony. The queen is asking to share this land with us for her children. So to us the treaty was an adoption ceremony. We adopted the queen's children. There were seven ceremonies given to us by the white buffalo calf woman, and one of them was an adoption ceremony. And the very first adoption was an adoption of one people by another people. That's what we did with at treaty, so the relationship between Canadians and Indigenous people living here is one of relations. And we have a word in Cree, "kiciwamanawak" that describes that relationship. There isn't an equivalent word in English 'cause it means all of us Cree are related to all of the queen's children, so plural to plural cousins. So the queen's children are my cousins.

Song: "Adoption."

As long as the grass grows
We all travel this broken road
As long as the sun shines
We can fix this, we still have time
As long as the river flows
We can wash our hands of the old
As long as the wind blows
I still hold on to the dream of hope

Music underscoring continues.

ANGEL: I just got outta treatment. And I happened to be in the place where Colten Boushie was murdered by Gerald Stanley. Biggar. It was after the trial. And to be in that environment I felt like I was a target.

I was around White farmers and I went to an AA meeting and uh I was the only First Nation there. And I was scared for my life. An' I thought farmers were gonna come to the treatment centre and drag me out and kill me. But I also knew that I was healing. I thought well, I'm just gonna walk into the enemy's camp and I'm gonna be myself and live and so I did. *(laughs)* Heh heh. And as frustrated and as angry as I was towards the people in that area, they were kind . . . and they were loving, and they were trustworthy. The farmers that I had met, they've hugged me and they have compassionately spoken kind and loving words toward me, and I was able to do the same thing back. But when I felt the prejudice or the racism . . . I spoke up about it aand everybody sat there and they thought about it and there was no reaction on it and it felt good. It felt like I was freeing my soul from a death that wasn't supposed to happen.

I spent seven weeks in the enemy's camp to find love and-and com-passion there. Reality is . . . that if you forgive . . . it frees you from being bitter, it frees you from wanting to murder the other person

that un—that goes away and gets to walk. And it makes you feel like
. . . It felt-it felt like a relationship was being built.

Scene 13—Forgiveness

Fast version.

Let's change the story, let it go
It's time for us to take control
So our kids don't have to know
All this fear that we own

Music out.

Scene 14—Needs

MICHAEL, *forties, White.*

Piano underscoring.

MICHAEL: If you want a canary in the coal mine it's the kids right?
Everybody's raised the flag an' . . . says we're on Treaty 6 territory.
What are the actions right? What does reconciliation look like?

When I go to Pleasant Hill . . . Park an' I . . . with uh summer snack
program and sit down an make Cheez Whiz sandwiches and nut
butter sandwiches an' . . . like kids come up and point out the bread
an' I make em a sandwich and you look em in the eye and you think
. . . they're just like they're filled with . . . same—like hopes and
dreams an' . . . as any other . . . person but . . . live in a society where
they have to go through every day wondering do I—do people
care about me? Do I-do I belong? After Colten Boushie, the Gerald
Stanley acquittal . . . you think okay, so if I'm a young Indigenous
person . . . growing up in this province, and not only am I hearing and imagining the images of this kid being shot but I'm also
hearing all of the . . . commentary about what people think about

people like me. It's just devastating right? I mean THAT empathy was
... really not there, right?

JEFF, sixties, White.

JEFF: If I was talking te-te kids at school, especially in the elementary years, I think I'd ask them two questions. First it'd be the
open-ended WHAT DO YOU NEED? What do you NEED from ME as
a citizen who wants better things for you? Secondly and this is
my curiosity about mentoring about uhm adult role models and
influences. WHO is the adult that makes you FEEL you can be the
best you?

ALICE, teens, Indigenous.

ALICE: What do I need to be my best? I need more time. More
time. I need some sort of balance in my life. In one of our teach-
ings w-we're taught in school, but I didn't learn this at home, is
called the Medicine Wheel teaching. It talks about . . . balance and
harmony and four elements being aligned so that a person can
be happy. *(cough) Hem* I feel like that's what I need. I need . . . balance. The Medicine Wheel te help me. *(cough) Hem* my mom isn't
at home. She's-she's she spends two weeks at Fort Mac. Sometimes
three weeks if she wants to make more money . . . an' she's only
source of income we have . . . an' my dad lives in the city but we
don't see each other often. He has another family I guess at home
he needs te look after. *(cough) Hmm* but sometimes he takes me out
for lunch. Although it would be nice to have both of them at home.
There's just me, my cousin who's a-a teen mom. So . . . I need te
help with her too.

Music continues under.

BOB, ten, Indigenous.

BOB: My name is Bob and I am ten.

JEFF: What do you NEED from ME as a citizen who wants better things for you?

BOB: I-I need a espiration and love te be the best. Espiration . . . to help me move on . . . Move on from the people who I—who don't care about you and hurt you. I'm lonely. 'Cause I am lonely. I need love because I am lonely. 'Cause nobody will help. 'Cause nobody will help me.

I live behind St. Paul's Hospital. Next door they're scary, I don't like them. First of all, one-one day I heard the window break next door. I dunno what from, but I-I think it's from something they did. It was scary. 'Cause . . . I didn't know what was happening and I thought it was like a gunshot.

JEFF: WHO is the adult that makes you FEEL you can be the best you?

BOB: My dad. 'Cause he's the closest one to me. Uh he . . . I've been living with him ever since I was born. 'Cause sometimes my mom goes to prison. He . . . he makes me feel nice and, sometimes when I go to school, he gives me treats. Yeah, like going to the movies or he buy me something. Yeah. Because I've been going to school-k-school early and more than my broders . . . I'm getting really emotional. (*laugh*) Heh. He helps me by saying-saying it's going to be okay and . . . to not-to not worry. That . . . that I'm—that I'm a good boy.

> *RONALD, sixties, Indigenous.*

RONALD: Tell some positive stories. We need five positive stories for every negative story because of the way that we're made. We all go back to cave man days. And when we were cave people, we had to pay attention to what was going on outside, and any danger that was around. So we're pre-programmed genetically to pay attention to anything negative, so we see or hear a negative news story on the television, we focus on it, instinctively focus on any negative story.

But those negative stories are killing us. To counteract that, we—
somewhere I read that we need five positive stories.

It starts with you and me
Sitting blissfully
And we all know within
The story's running thin

Sitting in the same sun as she grows
Seeing the same truth we all know
Watch it rise and feel the glow
It's time it's time it's time

Music out.

DALTON, fifties, Indigenous.

DALTON: I would just like to uh, acknowledge everybody here that
came tonight. Uhm . . . For you to take time out of yer, yer day
. . . an just to uh . . . sit here. To ME, ih—it says something about
YOU, as a person. I have uh, hope, for a better future. The only way
things are ever gonna get better, is uh, we need te talk about these
things . . . an' we need to uh, visit with one another an', get to know
one another . . . and uh, that's what I saw here tonight uh, even
though we don' know each other but, we-we came an' we sat an' we
listened an' . . . and uh, we need to do more a that.

DENNY, fifties, Indigenous.

DENNY: Truth. I was seeking truth. This is why I took the feather
in there. Through the eagle, we pray for all people. No madder
. . . where they come from . . . in all four directions . . . te this world
here, we pray for . . . for humanity. We pray for life.

Blackout.

The *Reasonable Doubt* Teacher Guide is the result of a collaboration between the play's co-creators—Joel Bernbaum, Lancelot Knight, and Yvette Nolan—and three Saskatchewan educators—Tracy Laverty, Dillon Person, and Sherry Van Hesteren. They all live and work in Treaty 6 Territory. The Saskatchewan Human Rights Commission and the Concentus Citizenship Education Foundation generously supported the project.

As a work of verbatim theatre, *Reasonable Doubt* is uniquely designed to allow audiences to collectively observe others engaged in conversations about race. The script and performance take people's intense, often hidden thoughts and feelings about race and embody them elsewhere—in the words on the page and the actors on the stage. This creates space for audience members and readers to:

a. reflect inwardly on how the play's voices echo and challenge their own;

b. talk together about how the play's speakers talk about race.

Reading the play together gives all involved the opportunity to channel the voices of fellow citizens who are both like and unlike them, in age, gender, race, experiences, and belief systems. As participants see, hear, feel, imagine, and remember through many different Is/eyes, they enter into what Willy Ermine describes as "ethical space": "The space offers a venue to step out of our allegiances, to detach from the cages of our mental worlds and assume a position where human-to-human dialogue can occur" (202).˙

Reasonable Doubt has incredible potential to support decolonial learning and community building—in the classroom and in professional learning. The guide offers materials and approaches that leaders of learning can use and adapt to sustain and deepen the work of Truth and Reconciliation in their own unique contexts.

---

*   Ermine, Willie. "The Ethical Space of Engagement." *Indigenous Law Journal*, vol. 6, no. 1, 2007, pp. 193–203.

All of the materials are available on the Concentus Citizenship Education Foundation website (www.concentus.ca). They include:

- introductory materials for leaders and teachers
- student viewing guide for *The Pass System*, directed by Alex Williams
- a timeline of events before, during, and after the trial of Gerald Stanley
- subject area materials for Drama, ELA, and Social Sciences (including History, Indigenous Studies, and Law)
- the *Reasonable Doubt* Film Series featuring themed interviews with Bernbaum, Knight, and Nolan—filmed and produced by Little Ox Film Company
- strategies for Teaching and Learning, including a Courageous Conversations Facilitation Guide

The *Reasonable Doubt* Teacher Guide is an evergreen resource—a living document that will grow and change over time to reflect the many ways that leaders and learners bring *Reasonable Doubt* to light and life in their communities throughout the province and country. We offer this guide with humility and excitement, in the hope that it will animate learning that is healing and transformative.

In the pages that follow, you will find samples from the guide. Head to the website to see the rest!

LESSON

1

OPENING QUESTIONS

- What does the term verbatim mean? (Watch *Reasonable Doubt* Video "Theme: Creating the Script: Audience, Artistry, Ethics, & Community— The Process: Audience, Artistry, and Ethics"
- Do we use this technique in our everyday lives?
- What are the advantages of this storytelling?
- What disadvantages does it have?

PROCESS

1. **Elements of Storytelling:** Provide examples and definitions for the following: Tempo/Pauses; Tone; Articulation; Diction; Expression (physical and verbal).

2. **Listen and Repeat:** With students in partners, use a variety of poetry and do the following activities to practice the above Elements of Storytelling. Student A reads one line, Student B listens and repeats, then Student B will read and Student A will listen and repeat. (Student A and Student B should have different poems from each other).

   a. Read each line very fast/very slow with random pauses between words.
   b. Read each line by over-enunciating consonant sounds/by mumbling and slurring your words.

   QUICK QUESTION: How can tone imply a bias? How might actors impose tone in their work that might express certain opinions even though the words may not?

   c. Read each line by adding levels of expression (i.e., listener interprets words by making them into movements; they perform it as if they can't stop smiling; announcing it to the entire world; whispering; gossip to your best friend; like you're playing a prank; and so on).

3. **Story Time:** Teacher demonstrates first by telling the class a story of a time where they persevered. Encourage strong listening here. Have students volunteer to retell the story. Students will rate performances with a thumbs up, sideways, or down on

MATERIALS:
- Poems for each student (there should be a variety).
- Journals and writing utensils.
- Space for students to spread out and move for certain activities.

accuracy of details, physicality, tone, etc. Students may try to make fun of the teacher. This is a teachable moment on honouring the story, the storyteller, and maintaining the integrity of the narrative.

a. Have students partner up and tell each other a story of a time where they persevered (ensure that they are choosing stories that they truly feel safe sharing with the entire class so they aren't putting themselves in compromising positions), and their partners will listen to their story and try to remember their movements and will retell the story to the entire class exactly how it was told. They should try to embody the character of their partner. Each student must share the story they were told. This is important for the entire class to practise taking the risk and sharing. Make sure there are no corrections of the story or coaching from the sidelines from the other student. Students can discuss the accuracy with their partner after everyone finishes. If students are struggling with coming up with a story, you may suggest to share a story that has not happened to them but they know about it, or the story of a character they read in a book or saw on a TV series that persevered and how that could be inspirational.

CLOSING ACTIVITY

Discuss: Was it easy to tell the story accurately? What were the easy parts to remember? What were the hard parts to remember? Why? (Show the *Reasonable Doubt* video "Theme: Creating the Script: Audience, Artistry, Ethics, & Community— Relationships: The Greatest Challenge & The Greatest Opportunity").

Journal Entry #1   In your own words, describe verbatim theatre and how this can be used as a tool to examine social justice issues in our communities. How can this type of theatre help communities develop empathy? What are the challenges of using this type of theatre?

For each scene in the play, the ELA resources provide before, during, and after prompts and scaffolds for leaders and learners. Learning tasks support participants to make their thinking visible and audible as they interpret and respond to the play. This formative assessment information allows teachers to perceive and respond to learners' affective and cognitive strengths and needs in "real time." Key concepts in social justice, anti-racist, and anti-oppressive learning are woven into the materials.

REASONABLE DOUBT

ACT 1
SCENE 8

PAGES 31–36

"IMMIGRANTS & PANHANDLERS"

JULIA	30s	CAUCASIAN
FORBES	40s	CAMEROONIAN
MOHAMMED	30s	PALESTINIAN
DEVON	30s	JAMAICAN
RICHARD	40s	AFGHAN
HAJESH	20s	CONGOLESE

BEFORE . . .

One of the speakers in this scene says that "within two weeks [of arriving in Saskatoon], almost every immigrant can figure out the hierarchy of the races [here]" (31). Do you think that there is a racial hierarchy, here, where you live? How do you know? How do you think someone new to here would "figure it out"?

DURING & AFTER . . .

1. In the first half of the scene (31–32), several immigrants share the sources of information that shape(d) their perceptions of Indigenous people. What are these sources? What do they learn and conclude from each one?

SPEAKER	SOURCE OF KNOWLEDGE?	WHAT THEY PERCEIVED, LEARNED, IMAGINED, BELIEVED?
FORBES		
MOHAMMED		
DEVON		
RICHARD		
HAJESH		

2. Sam speaks several times in the scene. What stereotype does he directly challenge?

3. What parts of his story does Clarence share with us? What do his words allow audience members to know and understand about him? to feel? to wonder?

4. Felix, Will, Anna, and Pamela then reflect on how they have been taught racism. What insight does each one share?

SPEAKER	SUMMARY OF SPEAKER'S MEMORY/THOUGHTS	WHAT THE SPEAKER REALIZES/SUGGESTS ABOUT RACISM
FELIX		
WILL		
ANNA		
PAMELA		

5. In the last page of the scene, Danny and Vihaan introduce some new ideas and questions. State these in your own words. How would you reply if they shared these ideas and questions in a conversation with you?

6. View the news report about the billboards Vihaan refers to:

https://saskatoon.ctvnews.ca/video?clipId=1160700&jwsource=em

Do you think that Vihaan would be satisfied by the explanation speakers in the video provide of the intent of the billboard? Why or why not?

7. The scene ends with a question and answer. The person who poses the question is Devon, a Jamaican man in his thirties. The person who answers it is Sam, an Indigenous person.

Is this the first time in the play, outside of the courtroom, that dialogue between an Indigenous person and a non-Indigenous person has occurred? What is the tone of their exchange—judgmental, caring, callous, earnest?

8. How would you describe the structure of the play thus far? Do you notice any of its ideas or elements shifting, gradually or suddenly? Is there a protagonist? An antagonist?

REASONABLE DOUBT
meets
THE BIG SIX HISTORICAL THINKING CONCEPTS

2 HISTORICAL THINKING CONCEPT 2: **EVIDENCE**

NOTE TO TEACHERS: Several interviews in the *Reasonable Doubt* Video Series will help students engage with the questions below!

HOW DO WE KNOW WHAT WE KNOW ABOUT THE PAST?

GUIDEPOST 1
History is an **interpretation** based on **inferences** made from primary sources. Primary sources can be accounts, but they can also be traces, relics, or records.
- What primary sources of evidence does the play contain?
- Is the play itself a primary source for historians today and in the future?

GUIDEPOST 2
Asking good questions about a source can turn it into evidence.
- What questions would an historian ask about this play as a potential source of historical evidence?

GUIDEPOST 3
Sourcing often begins before a source is read, with questions about **who** created it and **when** it was created. It involves inferring from the source the author's or creator's **purposes, values, and world view**, either conscious or unconscious.
- Who created this play? When was it created?
- What are the play's creators' purposes for the play?
- What values guided the creation of the play?
- There are three playwrights. They bring three related yet distinct histories and world views to their collaboration. What world view do they express together through the play?

concentus

GUIDEPOST 4

A source should be analyzed in relation to the **context of its historical setting:** the conditions and world views prevalent at the time in question.

- In what historical context was this play written?
- What conditions and world views were prevalent in Saskatchewan (and Canada) at the time of the killing of Colten Boushie and the trial of Gerald Stanley?

GUIDEPOST 5

Inferences from a source can never stand alone. They should always be **corroborated**—checked against other sources (primary or secondary).

- How did the playwrights invite Indigenous and non-Indigenous community members to corroborate interviewees' statements in the draft of the script of *Reasonable Doubt*?
- What did they do when a community member alerted them to an inaccuracy in the script (such as an omission or distortion)?
- How did interviewees serve both as sources of knowledge and corroborators of that same knowledge?
- What significant conclusions does the play suggest about race relations in Saskatchewan? What other primary and secondary sources can you consult to evaluate the validity of (one of the) play's conclusions?

COURAGEOUS CONVERSATIONS
FACILITATION PROCESS
by Sherry Van Hesteren

The *Reasonable Doubt* Teacher Resources include a Courageous Conversations Facilitation Guide.

In a sense, the play *Reasonable Doubt* is an extended courageous conversation. Engaging in the play invites participants to have many courageous conversations of their own!

In a courageous conversation, participants with diverse identities collaboratively explore the inequities which privilege some of them while oppressing others. Thus, every participant has a vested interest in the matter! Examining and altering the biases and bases of our selfhood and group identities in light of new knowledge requires great courage, hence the term "Courageous Conversations."

The Challenge: How can we, as educators and leaders, engage with critical and controversial issues in ways that optimize student and organizational learning and growth while minimizing harms?

By using facilitation processes and strategies which:

1. ensure that all participants have multiple ways and opportunities to express their ideas and points of view;
2. increase the number and diversity of points of view included, fairly represented, actively considered;
3. require active listening;
4. generate new questions that address newly discovered complexities;
5. result in shifts in thinking;
6. protect participants from unwanted exposure and personal attacks.

You can find the four-stage facilitation guide and Teacher Toolkit on the Concentus site.

concentus
CITIZENSHIP EDUCATION FOUNDATION
FONDATION D'ÉDUCATION À LA CITOYENNETÉ

Special Thanks

Philip Adams
Senator David Arnot
Alvin Baptiste
Debbie Baptiste
Judah Bernbaum
Mel Bernbaum
Maria Campbell
Charlie Clark
Kristen Dion
Melanie Doerr
Andrea Folster
Daxton and Kaliegha Knight
Lyndon Linklater
Bruce McKay
Jeremy Morgan
Joseph Naytowhow
Ashraf Gabriel Ogram
Marilyn Poitras
Laura Sackville
Priscilla Settee
Michael Shamata
Donnie Speidel
Verna St. Denis
Dara Hrytzak
Western Development Museum Collection, SK

Joel Bernbaum is an actor, director, playwright, journalist, and the founding artistic director of Sum Theatre. Born and raised in Saskatoon, Joel is the only child of a Buddhist mother and Jewish father. He is a graduate of the Canadian College of Performing Arts and Carleton University, where he did his master's thesis on verbatim theatre's relationship to journalism. With Sum Theatre, Joel created Saskatchewan's first free professional live Theatre in the Park. To date, over 50,000 people have participated in Sum Theatre's work. Joel's produced plays include *Operation Big Rock*, *My Rabbi* (with Kayvon Khoshkam), *Home Is a Beautiful Word*, and *Being Here: The Refugee Project*. Joel is currently an interdisciplinary Ph.D. student at the University of Saskatchewan, investigating the potential of theatre to strengthen cities. He is grateful to be the first Urjo Kareda Resident from Saskatchewan and the first Pierre Eilliott Trudeau Foundation Scholar from the University of Saskatchewan. Joel lives in Saskatoon with his son, Judah.

Lancelot Knight is a Plains Cree singer-songwriter from Saskatoon, Saskatchewan. He has toured in Germany, travelled to New Zealand, and across North America. Spanning genres and all forms of artistry, he also plays guitar for his father's band Chester Knight and the Wind, and has toured with Joey Stylez. Lancelot Knight recently co-created the play *Reasonable Doubt*.

Yvette Nolan is a playwright, dramaturg, and director. Her plays include *Annie Mae's Movement*, *The Unplugging*, and *The Birds*. She has been writer-in-residence at Brandon University, Mount Royal College, Saskatoon Public Library, and McGill University, as well as playwright-in-residence at the National Arts Centre. Born in Saskatchewan to an Algonquin mother and an Irish immigrant father and raised in Manitoba, Yvette lived in the Yukon and Nova Scotia before moving to Toronto, where she served as artistic director of Native Earth Performing Arts from 2003 to 2011. Her book *Medicine Shows* about Indigenous theatre in Canada was published in 2015. She lives in Saskatoon.